TIDES OF WAR

BOOK ONE
BLOOD IN THE WATER

36

C. Alexander Lon

SCHOLASTIC I

ISBN 978-0-545-66298-7

Copyright © 2014 by C. Alexander London
All rights reserved. Published by Scholastic Inc.
SCHOLASTIC and associated logos are trademarks and/or registered trademarks of Scholastic Inc.

2 11 10 9 8 7 6 5 4 3 2 1   14 15 16 17 18 19/0

d in the U.S.A.   40
inting, September 2014

To my mother, who is probably part fish.

PROLOGUE

THE surfers called it *dawn patrol*, and it was Cory's favorite time to surf with his little brother. The ocean sparkled gold in the first light of morning. The city behind the beach was just waking up, and the water was smooth as glass out beyond the breakers. The surf wasn't crowded like it would be a few hours from now.

Cory sat astride his surfboard, dangling his feet in the water, while Aaron lay on his back, an arm draped over his eyes. They bobbed gently as the swells off the Pacific rushed toward shore. Cory watched the sunrise. Aaron was twelve and had no interest in sunrises.

If he wasn't riding a wave or looking for the next one, he wanted to be sleeping.

Cory thought of his younger brother like some kind of surfing sea creature. All Aaron did was sleep and eat and surf and sleep some more.

Cory was envious. He hadn't been sleeping well at all lately. He had a full week off at home, but he wasn't finding it restful. He wasn't even *supposed* to be home right now, surfing with his little brother. The United States Navy had *sent* him home after the most humiliating day of his life: the day he quit training to become a part of the navy's Sea, Air, and Land teams, better known as the Navy SEALs. They were the toughest, most elite special forces operators in the world, and their training was the most difficult military training anyone had ever created.

He'd failed it.

Cory had made it through a month of the Basic Underwater Demolition/SEAL training, a series of grueling physical and mental tests. BUD/S trainees barely sleep, barely eat, and hardly ever get to clean themselves. They spend most of their time cold and wet and in pain.

He had been doing fine being miserable until the fourth week of training, the week they called *Hell Week*. That was when Cory reached his breaking point.

After twenty-hour days of being shouted at by instructors, running countless wet and sandy miles, and never sleeping more than four hours in a row, he knew he couldn't handle another week of the training, let alone another five months. And he'd been told that after the training, the life of a Navy SEAL was even harder. Could he really commit to spending his entire career feeling this horrible all the time?

At the end of Hell Week, he took his helmet liner to the little green sign with the bell next to it, set it down, and rang the bell three times. That was the signal that he had quit.

No one was looking at him when he did it, but he felt like all the eyes of everyone he'd ever known were on him, judging him, seeing that he was a failure. Cory wasn't the first to drop out and he knew he wouldn't be the last — eighty out of every hundred guys in BUD/S training drop out before it's over — but knowing that did nothing to lessen his shame.

He went home for a few days to recover, to collect himself and tell his friends and family he would not be a Navy SEAL.

He didn't know yet where the navy would assign him next, but he was pretty sure it would be a job that no one else wanted. He would receive his new assignment any day now. He wasn't so sure he would accept it. He thought about quitting the navy altogether.

"You ready to go in and get some breakfast?" Cory asked Aaron as they floated on the ocean.

His little brother didn't even turn his head. "You tired already, old man?"

Cory wasn't tired, he just didn't feel like having fun. It was too much work to enjoy himself when all he wanted to do was wallow in self-pity.

He made up an excuse. "I'm sick of choppy swells," he said. "There are nothing but bad breaks this morning."

Aaron sat up, paddled himself right next to his brother, and looked at him gravely. "There are no bad waves, Cory," Aaron told him. "Just bad surfers."

Cory sighed, then leaned over and shoved his younger brother right off his board.

"Bwah!" Aaron laughed, falling with a splash, and surfaced right beside Cory again. He shook his mess of blond curls out like a wet dog. Cory rubbed his own crew cut.

Aaron may still have had his hair, and he may have been twice the surfer that Cory was, but Cory's brief time in SEAL training had given him one advantage: He'd only been home a few days and his muscles were still ripped. What good was having a little brother if you couldn't show him who was boss from time to time?

He shoved Aaron under with one arm, counting to five before letting him go.

Aaron popped up, gasping. He looked up at Cory. "If the navy deploys you to the other side of the world, I'm totally taking your room."

Cory moved to shove him under again. Aaron flinched. Cory smiled and helped Aaron back onto his board. He didn't mention that he probably wasn't going anywhere, that he was probably quitting the navy.

"You know," Aaron said, looking away from his brother, like he did whenever he said anything important to him. "Most guys wouldn't survive a day in SEAL training."

Cory didn't know what to say to that. He just shrugged. Then he actually felt himself tearing up with regret.

One day or four weeks. There was no difference if you quit before you finished. You weren't good enough to be a Navy SEAL.

Without another word about it, Aaron flipped around on his board and paddled into the surf. He called back over his shoulder: "Try to keep up, sailor!"

Cory was grateful. He didn't want to cry in front of his little brother.

He lay down on his board and swam after Aaron. With a few sweeping strokes, he was paddling alongside.

A big swell rose behind them and Cory felt that rush as it pushed them forward, raising the tail of their boards, speeding them up. Aaron glanced over his shoulder at Cory, gave him a nod, and together, like there was a string connecting them, they popped up to their feet, driving the back of their boards down into the wave as it crested, and cruising along its face.

Cory was just behind Aaron. He felt the beautiful pressure of the wave, the air across his shaved head, the splash of the salt water against his face. He watched the muscles on Aaron's back to see when his brother was going to turn up into the wave, to cut back, to drop to the bottom of the trough and zip up it again, to jump and grab the board in the air.

Cory tried to keep up, but Aaron could do tricks Cory couldn't even think of. The best he could do was to keep his eyes fixed on his little brother and try not to crash into him.

He was so focused on not wiping out that he didn't see the shark's fin slicing the wave beside Aaron until it was too late.

Time slowed down.

As Aaron turned to pull another trick, the shark's jaws rose from the foaming ocean and clamped around his leg. The large gray body twisted like a corkscrew and snatched Aaron from the board, dragging him into the water. Aaron's surfboard snapped free of its tether and spun away on the wave, empty.

Time sped up again as the wave smashed over Cory, knocking him from his board. He was upside down. The surf roared in his ears like screaming, or maybe it *was* screaming, his own screaming or his brother's screaming.

Bubbles and foam all around him. He struggled to tell which way was up.

Follow the bubbles, he thought. *Bubbles rise.*

He clawed for the surface, broke into the light with a gasp of air, and shouted, "Aaron! Aaron!"

He couldn't see anything through the foam and the rolling waves. Another wave came down on him, knocked him under again. He popped up, spitting and coughing.

He looked right, to the beach, where he saw people shouting and pointing. He spun to his left, dove forward, and came up past the breaking waves, where he saw Aaron, thrashing in a cloud of red water.

Cory swam toward them as fast as he could, his brain running on autopilot, the rush of adrenaline overtaking him.

Aaron was frantically punching the shark's nose, but it wasn't letting go. Its jaws gripped Aaron around the waist now and the giant fish shook from side to side, tossing the boy back and forth like a rag doll. His face was pale and the ocean around him was red.

Aaron's blood in the water was like a ringing dinner bell for any other sharks in the area. A shark can smell one drop in over a million drops of seawater. If more showed up, if a feeding frenzy began, there'd be little hope of getting out of the water alive.

When Cory reached the shark, he threw himself onto the great white's side, hugging the beast and trying to pull it upright with all his strength. If the shark's gills were turned in the wrong direction, the shark wouldn't be able to breathe and, with any luck, it would let go of Aaron.

What would happen *after* the shark let go, Cory hadn't considered.

The shark did let go, but it thrashed wildly as it did, and its tail smacked Cory across the face, twisting him around. He saw the red-blue sky above, still colored with dawn, and then he plunged down into the red-blue water below. The wind was knocked out of him.

Cory watched as, with one more flick of its powerful tail, the shark vanished into the dark below. He looked up and saw the waves overhead. He saw Aaron, floating sideways in a sea of red, his head limp in the water, blond hair floating out around him, lit by the sun above so it looked like a halo.

Cory felt so tired; too tired to swim. The surface was just so far away. He needed to rest. He'd rest and then . . . then he'd find out if Aaron was okay. Someone would tell him. Surely someone would tell him. . . .

His vision faded and he knew he was drowning, knew his mind was shutting down beneath the waves, and he didn't even have the strength to panic. In the deep beyond he could swear he saw the eyes of a thousand sharks fixed on him, racing up, slicing through the water to get to him, but he also heard loud, sharp whistles and clicks, strange sounds from the deep, and they were coming closer.

Something bumped him from below. Something powerful. It pushed him up, shoving him toward the surface.

Just before his vision went black, in the dimness of the bloody ocean, Cory tried to make out the creature.

All he could see were two big black eyes, a pointed snout, and what, in the chaos of his half-drowned mind, looked like a giant smile. And all around him, a chorus of whistling, the most beautiful song Cory had ever heard.

01:
FLYING FISH

CORY woke with a start.

His shirt was soaked. He tasted salt water on his lips.

He'd been having that nightmare again, clear as the day it had happened, when he and Aaron had barely survived a shark attack in the early morning surf. The day his life had been saved by a pod of wild dolphins.

Cory had cried out in his sleep, but no one else on board the giant C-130 cargo plane seemed to have noticed. The veterinarian and the technicians were asleep in their seats. The technical representative, who was a civilian dolphin trainer from the university, slept in a cot near the cockpit, and all the other petty officers and seamen had sprawled about the cabin wherever there was room.

The rest of the plane was filled with supplies — rigid-hull inflatable boats, medical equipment, freezers full of fish, floating pontoons, inflatable pools, and directly across from Cory, the mobile transport pen: a rectangular water tank with a harness suspended inside it. Inside that harness was an eight-foot-long, six-hundred-pound Atlantic bottlenose dolphin named Kaj.

Suddenly, salt water splashed across Cory's face and he heard the dolphin's repeated *click click click*, just like in his dream.

"Thanks, Kaj," Cory said, wiping his face off on a dry corner of his drab olive T-shirt. The dolphin clicked at him, amused.

Kaj was one of the thirty-five Atlantic bottlenose dolphins in the United States Navy's Marine Mammal Program. He was assigned to the program's MK 6 Fleet System, or *Mark 6*, as they called it. Mark 6 was a specialized unit of dolphins, sea lions, and human handlers, trainers, and support staff, who could deploy anywhere in the world within seventy-two hours to guard ships in port, search for underwater explosives, and stop swimmers from staging attacks from the sea. The dolphins were like the police dogs of the ocean.

Cory was Kaj's handler and Kaj was Cory's partner. They knew each other as well as a human and a dolphin could.

The navy took the well-being of its dolphins very seriously, which was why there were over twenty people on board this cargo plane to look after just one dolphin. There were cameras pointing at Kaj's tank, and there were all kinds of equipment in the water to record every sound the dolphin made. There were also buckets of fish in coolers and even more fish in the freezers they were hauling to the other side of the world.

While enlisted humans ate whatever tasteless, mass-produced military chow the navy decided to serve in the mess deck, Kaj got to eat the highest quality mackerel, smelt, and herring that money could buy, and he ate twenty pounds of it every day.

Cory stood up to feed Kaj a piece now, which Kaj ate cheerfully. Sometimes it seemed like Cory's main job was chopping fish for Kaj. He often felt more like a seafood chef than a soldier.

"Thanks for waking me up," Cory said. Even though he knew dolphins didn't really understand English, Cory never forgot to thank the dolphin.

He gave Kaj another chunk of fish, and then wrote the two pieces down on a chart by the tank. As Kaj's handler, he had to keep track of everything. When he wasn't actually working with the dolphin, he was doing paperwork about the dolphin.

Kaj made a clicking noise to get Cory's attention again. He and Kaj had their own ways of communicating — hand gestures and commands, rewards of toys or fish, clicks and whistles and fin movements. Cory had even taught Kaj how to high-five. Now Kaj opened his mouth wide, revealing his long row of razor-sharp teeth and his big pink tongue. Cory knew what that meant.

"Oh, is that why you woke me up?" Cory said. "And here I thought you were just worried about me."

Kaj slapped his flukes — the fins at the back of his tail — on the water, which Cory had learned was his way of making a request. Cory laughed, but did what Kaj wanted him to do.

He reached into the dolphin's mouth and scratched his tongue.

Kaj rocked back and forth, left to right, enjoying the tongue scratching immensely. Scratching Kaj's tongue was just like scratching a dog behind its ears, except a lot wetter . . . and with a lot more teeth.

Sometimes Cory wondered who was the handler and who was being handled. He fed Kaj by hand, after all, not the other way around. He responded to Kaj's wants and needs as best he could, and Kaj did his best to make his wants and needs known. He supposed Kaj had trained him as much as he had trained Kaj.

Not everyone could so easily reach into the mouth of a six-hundred-pound ocean mammal to scratch its tongue, but Cory wasn't afraid of his dolphin. Kaj's face showed what to all the world looked like a giant grin. The famous dolphin smile.

The smile was an illusion. It was just the way a dolphin's jaw was shaped, but it was the memory of that smile that had led him here, to the night watch over Kaj on this cargo plane above the Pacific Ocean.

It was the memory of that smile that had made Cory want to be a dolphin handler. Cory had learned that a pod of wild dolphins had scared off the great white shark that morning in the surf with his brother, one year ago.

After the attack, Cory had lost consciousness underwater, but a wild dolphin had pushed him up to the surface with its nose and shoved him toward shore. Another had dragged Aaron to safety. A lifeguard then hauled both brothers to the beach and gave Cory CPR.

When Cory came to on the beach, he saw red marks in the sand where Aaron had been carried ashore. His brother had lost a lot of blood before being loaded onto an ambulance. Cory had to go to the hospital, too, to get stitches on his head where the shark's tail had smacked him, but he was back on his feet by that same afternoon.

Aaron, on the other hand, spent three days in a coma. No one knew if he would pull through or not. He had a huge bandage on his right side, where the great white had taken a chunk out of him. He'd been skinny to begin with. He didn't have a lot of flesh to lose.

Cory and his parents never left Aaron's side at the hospital, and when he came out of the coma, the first thing Aaron did was ask if Cory was okay.

"I'm right here," Cory said.

"You saved me," Aaron told him, his voice barely a whisper.

"I'm your big brother," Cory said. "It's my job."

Aaron grabbed his hand. "You fought off a shark."

Cory shrugged. "I had some help. A pod of dolphins."

"Dolphins?" Aaron asked.

"Dolphins," Cory said.

"Cool," Aaron said with a weak smile.

His mother cried, and both boys blushed. Aaron rolled his eyes so Cory could see, like he was saying, *Jeez, Mom, it was just a great white shark attack. Chill out.*

When Cory returned to the naval base in San Diego to report for duty, he requested a transfer to the Marine Mammal Program. If he was going to stay in the navy, he wanted to work with dolphins.

Only a few weeks later, his transfer orders came through, and Cory began his new job in the navy. For the next year, he spent his mornings chopping fish and cleaning tanks, and his afternoons studying dolphin behavior and biology. He spent his nights running and working out, staying fit.

In the protected waters of San Diego Bay at Naval Base Point Loma, he worked with Kaj, teaching him to obey commands and hand signals, and to identify objects underwater, like torpedoes and undersea mines. They practiced catching unauthorized swimmers, which involved sailors acting in the role of enemy scuba divers, and they played and got to know each other.

In the wild, dolphins use something called *echolocation* to hunt and to navigate their environments. It works like the sonar that the navy uses on-board submarines, but far more advanced. Dolphins make a series of clicks and whistles that travel through the water and bounce off distant objects, coming back to them and drawing a picture in sound. They can spot fish for hunting and scout out terrain with this "bio-sonar." They can also find other dolphins and communicate over long distances.

It was Cory's job — along with that of the other handlers, the civilian technical advisors, and the rest of the dolphin support staff — to explore the ways these amazing dolphin skills could be used to help the United States Navy.

As the months went by, he learned how to get Kaj to pick different objects off the seafloor, objects that would look identical to human eyes, but that were different on the inside. Some were solid and some were hollow. Some were dangerous and some were safe. Some were valuable — million-dollar pieces of equipment — and some were random junk.

To Kaj, it didn't matter. He found what he was asked to find and he got rewarded with fish or toys or, his favorite, tongue scratching.

Cory and Kaj became the most talented dolphin team in the navy's arsenal.

Cory thought that if everyone was impressed by Kaj, they wouldn't notice how scared Kaj's handler was. Cory did everything he could to stay on the boat and on the dock while his dolphin worked. He made up excuses — family commitments, too much paperwork, a sore back — anytime the guys he worked with invited him to go surfing. Even though he knew it was unlikely he'd ever be near another shark attack again in his life, even though he knew that sharks don't naturally eat people, and even though he knew he was in the United States Navy and could hardly avoid the ocean forever, he was still terrified of what lurked beneath the waves.

The nightmares about that terrible day with Aaron never stopped.

Now his commanders had chosen him for a top secret mission. He and his dolphin team had been ordered to fly out to a naval base in South Korea. There they would transport the dolphin onto the USS *Stokes* for deployment somewhere in the Sea of Japan, where they would receive further instructions.

He'd looked up the Sea of Japan on the Internet as soon as they'd received their orders: It was home to at least 124 species of shark, and whatever the navy needed them to do, Cory was sure they would be doing it in the open water that those sharks called home.

He really hoped no one on board the ship would notice how much that terrified him.

02:
DOLPHINS, SAILORS, AND SEALS

THE USS *Stokes* was a guided missile destroyer, which meant that it was one of the most heavily armed ships in the United States Navy. It could launch guided antiaircraft missiles, antisubmarine missiles, and sea-to-surface Tomahawk missiles. It had an antiship Harpoon missile system, a Mark 34 Artillery Gun System, and one of the most advanced radar and sonar arrays in the world. It was designed for stealth capabilities and high speeds.

All these weapons systems, radar systems, and stealth systems were in place for one reason and one reason only: war.

The USS *Stokes* was a battle-ready warship.

And now it had a dolphin team.

As the rest of the Marine Mammal Program staff began unloading all the dolphin equipment onto the tarmac in the early morning light, Cory wondered what such an advanced destroyer could need with him and Kaj. He wondered why no one had told them what they'd be doing yet, or why they'd had to land the cargo plane at this remote base where the destroyer was docked, before the sun came up, and unload "double-time."

He had to remind himself that it wasn't his job to know. It was his job to get the dolphin set up on board safely, and to work with others to make sure Kaj *stayed* safe. Safe and healthy.

Dr. Morris was the army veterinarian assigned to their unit, and she immediately claimed space in a cargo hold of the *Stokes* for a mobile medical clinic, Kaj's own private hospital at sea. She had a specially designed gurney with three padded sides and hooks to attach it to a crane, so she could wheel Kaj around easily.

While they were at sea, the dolphin would get daily checkups from the doctor. She had scanners and syringes, a refrigerator filled with medicines and vitamins, and a whole team of navy sailors to follow her orders, even though she was an army doctor and the navy and the army didn't always get along . . . especially during football season.

The head dolphin trainer, Noah Hankins, was a civilian, but an expert in dolphin care and behavior, and everyone listened when he spoke. Even though Noah's official title was "technical advisor," and even though he had no rank in the United States Navy, he was still Cory's boss, and Cory waited now for his instructions.

In the meantime, Cory stood beside Kaj's transport tank and rubbed the dolphin's head. Kaj had noticed all the activity around him and had become agitated. Transport was hard on a dolphin, and the moments of transition from one place to another were especially stressful.

It reminded Cory of grade school, when it was time to go from reading class to recess. Recess was way better than reading class, and all the kids would get wild a few minutes before it was actually time to go outside. The teacher would try to line them up, and if they didn't listen, she'd get mad and yell and sometimes they wouldn't get to go to recess at all because of how they had behaved. It wasn't anyone's fault, though. Sometimes kids got excited, and sometimes teachers got stressed out about it.

Everyone on the MK 6 dolphin team was excited now, running around, unloading frozen fish and setting up equipment, and that stressed Kaj out.

Cory knew that dolphins don't react well to stress. It could be very harmful to a dolphin, damaging his liver and his heart. It could make him sick.

Cory had to get Kaj to relax.

He rubbed Kaj and poured cool water over him. He bobbed his head up and down, as if nodding *yes*, so that Kaj could imitate him. The harness inside the transport tank rocked when Kaj nodded back vigorously.

Cory gave him a small chunk of fish to tell him he was doing fine. Kaj was just like Cory's little brother,

Aaron: No matter how stressed out he was, he could always eat.

One morning over breakfast, two months after the shark attack, Aaron had sat at their kitchen table, devouring a plate of bacon and eggs. He shoveled the food into his face like it was going to run away if he didn't eat it fast. He didn't even close his mouth as he chewed.

"You in a race?" Cory asked him.

"I gotta get to the beach before school," Aaron said, and Cory couldn't believe his ears.

"You're . . . you're surfing again?"

Aaron nodded, shoving another forkful of scrambled eggs into his mouth.

"I can't believe you'd get right back in the water," Cory said.

Aaron scoffed at his big brother's worries. "It's, like, basic math. Sharks never attack people. Well, *almost* never. So, that I got attacked was, like, a one-in-a-million chance, you know? Getting attacked again would be like winning the lottery twice in a row. Nobody wins the lottery twice in a row."

"The lottery gives you money when you win," said Cory. "It doesn't try to eat you."

"The shark wasn't trying to eat me," Aaron objected. "*You* told me that about sharks, like, ages ago. They don't eat people. This one was just confused. He took a bite. He didn't swallow."

"So what if you run into another confused shark? One who takes a bigger bite?"

Aaron shrugged. "You can be afraid if you want to," he said. "But you can't let being afraid stop you from doing what you want."

Cory looked down at the table and pressed the crumbs with his index finger so they stuck. He lifted them up, looked at them, brushed them off with his thumb. How'd his little brother get to be so wise? He was like a tween Yoda, if Yoda had been a surfer. Maybe almost dying gave Aaron more wisdom than most twelve-year-olds had. Or maybe everyone was this wise when they were twelve, but growing up made them forget.

Suddenly, Noah was at Cory's side, snapping him back from his memories to the work in front of him. "You'll be in charge of getting Kaj on board," Noah said, understanding the special bond between the handler and the dolphin. He nodded toward an officer who stood beside him. "Lieutenant Brown has Kaj's pool set up in the cargo hold, and he's providing a team of sailors to assist you."

"Whatever else you need, just say the word," Lieutenant Brown added.

"Thank you, sir," Cory said, snapping to attention. He gave the officer a salute. The officer glanced at the name stitched onto Cory's shirt just above his heart.

"At ease, McNab," Lieutenant Brown said, using Cory's last name. "And welcome aboard."

Lieutenant Brown was the executive officer — XO for short — of the USS *Stokes*, the second-in-command behind the captain. He was about a million ranks above Cory in the United States Navy, and that he'd come down to welcome them was a big deal. Cory wasn't sure what it meant, but he knew that people were paying attention to him now. It wouldn't just be him and his team doing their own thing. He'd have the eyes of the whole ship on him.

Noah and the lieutenant disembarked, and they were immediately replaced by a group of sailors. This was the team Lieutenant Brown had promised, ready to take their orders from Cory. He was only a petty officer. He wasn't used to giving commands to anyone other than his dolphin.

The sailors stared at Cory, waiting for their instructions.

"Okay," he told them, clapping his hands together. He thought again about elementary school. His fifth-grade teacher had always clapped before she made an announcement. Cory hadn't thought about that in years. He was nervous.

"We need to wheel Kaj's mobile tank down the ramp," he explained. "Then we'll attach it to the back of that jeep there and drive him over to the ship. We'll wheel him from the jeep right into the cargo hold where his pool's been set up. Is there a winch on board to hoist him into the pool?"

The sailors told him there was.

"Great," said Cory. "We have to move slowly and steadily, so we don't worry him. He'll be watching and he'll be listening, and he hears more than you think, so don't shout or curse or do anything that could make him think he's not safe."

"Don't curse?" one of the sailors scoffed. Cursing was one of the things navy sailors did best. They were famous for it.

"That's right," Cory said. "Kaj doesn't like curse words."

"Aye aye," one of the sailors said cheerily, and Cory wondered if he was being sarcastic. These were sailors stationed on a warship. Did they resent having to take orders from the guy with the dolphin? And why was Cory so worried about it? Did he think they could see how scared he was? Scared of failure, scared of embarrassment, scared of the ocean itself . . .

He clenched his jaw and thought of Aaron, riding the waves only months after a shark had nearly killed him. If Aaron could do *that*, surely Cory could do *this*. Fear would not control him.

"Let's get moving!" Cory told the sailors.

They got Kaj out into the morning air, Cory keeping him wet and comfortable as they moved. In just a few minutes, they'd hooked Kaj's tank to the jeep and made their way across the base and on board the *Stokes*.

Just like Noah had said, a large rigid inflatable pool, about ten feet deep, was set up in the cargo hold. It was filled with seawater, filtered and temperature controlled for Kaj's comfort. When the ship was underway, a ring of netting would be zipped up around the rim of the pool so the dolphin wouldn't accidentally jump out or fall out in rough seas.

Cory poured another pitcher of cool water over Kaj and rubbed his back. "Home away from home," he said, not caring that the others could hear him talking to his dolphin. They were doing their jobs well and he was doing his and that was all that mattered.

As much as Cory dreaded when they would have to go out into the open ocean, he imagined Kaj would be thrilled about it. All these water tanks and inflatable pools were just hotel rooms as far as the dolphin was concerned. The ocean was his true home.

They used the crane to lift Kaj up from his mobile tank by the harness, and for a moment the dolphin hung suspended in the air between the cart and the pool, his tail hanging off the back of the harness, his head poking from the front. One of his eyes locked on Cory below. Kaj opened his mouth for a tongue scratching, but Cory couldn't reach. Then Kaj snapped his mouth shut, loudly. It was a dolphin sign of aggression. Kaj did not like being in the air.

"Lower him in!" Cory shouted.

"No shouting!" one of the sailors mocked. Cory glared at him, but quickly turned his focus back to the crane operator, who was taking his cues from Cory's hand gestures.

They got Kaj into the pool and unhooked his

harness, and Kaj gave a powerful flick of his tail. He circled the pool three times, rolled onto his back, and used his pectoral fins to splash around the edge, soaking all of the sailors. He let out a series of whistles that was like his signature, the way he identified himself to other dolphins in the ocean.

Cory thought the newly soaked sailors would be angry, but they all laughed and applauded Kaj's show. That gave Cory an idea. He raised his arm up to get Kaj's attention, then made a gesture with his hand, dropped his arm, and whistled twice. Kaj understood.

The dolphin did a small breach of the surface, and sliced into the pool with a flip. Then he sped around the edge as fast as he could, and stood upright in the water, using his powerful tail to "walk" backward on the surface while clapping with his flippers. The sailors took his cue and clapped for him.

Kaj squealed and dove back in, swimming around the edge again with one flipper up for high fives from all the laughing sailors, who stood on tiptoe to reach his fin. He was showing off. Already, the men and women aboard the warship *Stokes* were impressed with Cory's dolphin.

Cory smiled.

Except then he noticed a group of eight guys at the far end of the cargo hold, watching Kaj's display with stern faces. They all had arms about as thick as Cory's head, some of them covered in tattoos. Their muscles bulged against their camouflage utility uniforms, and two of them even had beards, which was against navy regulations.

In the center of the group stood a clean-cut guy with a shaved head. He kept his arms crossed and stood unmoving while the others whispered in his ears. He wore wraparound sunglasses even though they were inside, and he did not crack a smile, even as the others chuckled at whatever was being whispered.

Cory was sure they were laughing at him and at his dolphin, and he was also sure he knew who these guys were. He saw a cloth patch sewn onto their camouflage: an anchor crossed with a trident and an old flintlock pistol. It was the insignia of the Special Warfare Operator Badge.

These guys were Navy SEALs.

One of the sailors next to Cory noticed him looking at them. "Keep your distance from those guys," he told Cory. "They're DEVGRU."

Cory didn't know what DEVGRU meant, and the sailor saw the confusion on his face.

"SEAL Team Six," the guy said, which was their more common name, even though it was no longer their official name. SEAL Team Six was the most top secret and most elite of all the SEAL teams. They were the best of the best. "They just got here last night," the sailor added.

Cory swallowed and looked back at Kaj, contentedly rolling around in his pool of cool water. Now he really had to wonder why they had been deployed to the USS *Stokes*. Why would the navy call up a dolphin team led by a SEAL training dropout at the same time they called up the most capable fighting unit in the world?

Kaj had only ever worked in the waters of San Diego Bay, and Cory had never been on a warship before. He suddenly doubted that he and Kaj were ready for whatever was in store for them. Well, maybe Kaj was ready . . . but Cory?

He was still the guy who'd failed SEAL training. No dolphin tricks could make up for that.

03:
TRAINING DAY

"WE'RE going to do some training from the RHIB today, McNab," Noah told Cory as they sat together in the mess deck early the next morning. Cory shoved a forkful of dry scrambled eggs into his mouth and nodded, but his heart thudded against his rib cage so loudly that he was sure Kaj could hear it all the way on the other end of the steel ship. He was wide-awake and totally alert, even though it was five in the morning.

RHIB stood for rigid-hull inflatable boat, and it was the standard vehicle for the dolphin team, but Cory had only ever used one in port within the confines of the naval base or in the nearby waters of San Diego Bay. He'd never been out in the open ocean. He thought again of all those sharks that called the Sea of Japan home. He thought of Kaj, held in his little pool, suddenly freed in the open water. The navy had never had a dolphin fail to return to his handler . . . but what if Kaj was the first? What if the call of the wild was too much for the dolphin to resist?

A thousand and one doubts raced through Cory's head, but he did his best to keep eating and listening to Noah tell him what he needed to know for the day's work. He shifted in his seat, the padded blue vinyl of the bench squeaking slightly. The benches were attached to the tables, just like in school cafeterias, except they were padded so that in rough seas, no one would crack his head open if he fell on one. Cory didn't know why they were blue, though, the same blue as the floor tiles beneath his feet. Overhead, fluorescent lights buzzed, tubes and pipes and conduits running every which way.

Cory realized he was looking all over the place, looking everywhere but at his boss. It would make his nervousness pretty obvious. He met Noah's eyes. "I'm looking forward to getting out on the water with Kaj," he said.

"You'll have some extra company on board," Noah told him. "I'll be there to advise, along with the driver. And we're going to have a special guest observing our methods." Noah pulled out a small notebook from his shirt pocket to check what he'd written down. "Master Chief Landon Charles," he said, closing the notebook and sliding it back into his pocket. He leaned forward and whispered. "He's a SEAL Team squad leader."

Cory nodded, remembering the stern guy with the shaved head. His blood ran like ice in his veins. He'd be sharing a small boat with the man.

"Do you know our mission?" Cory asked his boss.

Noah shook his head. "I don't have security clearance to know. It's classified. I won't be going with you on the mission itself. The XO told me: No civilians."

Cory tried to keep his hand steady. Training with the SEALs, and no civilians on their mission. That had to mean they expected trouble. Shooting-type trouble.

Cory didn't like the idea of involving Kaj in combat. It was one thing to use a dolphin for search and recovery; it was another to involve a dolphin in a gunfight. And there was another nagging thought in his mind. If there was shooting, there would be blood. And if there was blood, there would be sharks.

"Let's get to it," Noah said. "We only have today for training."

Cory cleared his plastic tray with half his eggs still on it. He wasn't hungry anymore.

■ ■ ■

The sun had just begun to peek over the horizon when they got Kaj and their rigid-hull inflatable boat into the water, lowered from cranes on the weather deck of the USS *Stokes*.

Kaj swam around the small boat's hull, rolling and twirling in a corkscrew as he swam. He popped to the surface for a breath through his blowhole, then dove into the dark water and vanished from sight.

Cory peered over the edge, but there was nothing

visible. In his mind he pictured a great white bursting from the water in front of him, snatching him in its jaws and dragging him down forever. He sat back suddenly, sweat already pouring down his face. He watched the water and waited for Kaj to return.

And waited.

And waited.

Finally, Kaj broke the surface again, just off the stern of the boat. His head popped out of the water, his small dark eyes flashing mischief and his face holding that perpetual dolphin grin.

"Enjoying yourself?" Cory asked. He made a hand gesture, and Kaj jumped from the water and slid on his belly onto a flat gray pad, like a wrestling mat, that was laid out on the back of the boat. That's where the dolphin would ride on their mission . . . whatever their mission might be.

The mat was divided into three sections. The outer two could be folded up together to make a triangle, like a padded tent, which would keep Kaj in the shade and help prevent him from bouncing out if the water got rough. For now, they left the mat open. The seas were smooth and the sun wasn't yet blazing.

Cory sat beside Kaj in the hull of the boat and rubbed the dolphin's side, and Kaj clicked and whistled contentedly. At Cory's feet were a covered bucket of fish and another covered bucket of some of Kaj's favorite toys. There were markers and beacons and other search and recovery tools strapped around the hull, and a stick extending off the side with a ratty baseball stuck to the end of it.

Kaj's signal. When the dolphin went out searching, he'd tap the baseball to tell Cory that he'd found what he'd been sent to find. It was amazing that they could bob in the water beside a multibillion-dollar navy destroyer loaded with millions of dollars worth of top secret equipment, but the mission they were about to go on relied on a six-dollar baseball and a grinning dolphin who liked to give high fives.

Noah sat to Cory's left, a waterproof camera in his hands, a whistle around his neck, and a binder full of checklists in his lap. The boat's driver stood at the wheel toward the front, facing forward, where a tarp covered some mysterious object, and Master Chief Landon Charles of SEAL Team Six stood beside the driver, facing Cory, Noah, and Kaj. His eyes were still hidden behind dark sunglasses, and he seemed unamused by Kaj's antics.

The driver wasn't their regular boat driver, the one who'd flown over with them. This was a guy neither Noah nor Cory knew. He was one of Landon's men, another SEAL. He wore a compact machine gun on his back, the strap wrapped tightly around his chest. Landon also had a submachine gun strapped to him. It was the first time Cory had worked with Kaj with weapons on board. He wondered what kind of trouble the SEALs imagined they might get into.

"All right, sailor," Landon shouted to Cory as the driver started the motor. "Last night we dropped a piece of equipment somewhere in these waters. We're told that your fish can find it."

Cory wanted to correct Landon. A dolphin is *not* a fish. The Atlantic bottlenose dolphin is an aquatic mammal of the cetacean order, which also includes whales and porpoises. As mammals they breathe air, give birth to live babies, whom they feed with milk, and they are warm-blooded, just like people. Dolphins aren't hairy like a lot of mammals, but they do have tiny hair follicles all over their bodies.

Other than their shape and the fact that they spend most of their lives below the surface of the water, they aren't really anything like fish. They *eat* fish — tons of fish — but they are so *not* fish themselves.

Instead of correcting the SEAL like he wanted to, however, Cory nodded. "Dolphins have advanced bio-sonar. If we can show him what he's looking for, he can find it."

"We need to get some distance from the *Stokes* first," Landon said. The driver guided them away from the ship and accelerated into open water. Another small boat came zipping out behind them, and Cory saw that the other six Navy SEALs were on board it. All of them had their guns with them, too.

Cory focused on Kaj, rubbing him and splashing water on him. Kaj opened his mouth to get a tongue scratching, which Cory provided. It kept him from thinking too much about the task ahead.

After speeding out for about forty minutes, the driver slowed the engine and Landon took the tarp off the object at the front. He revealed a black minisubmarine, about the size of a person, covered in a completely smooth black material that did not look like any metal Cory had ever seen before.

"What is that?" Cory asked.

"What you are seeing is classified top secret," Landon told them. "You don't need to know what it is, just that we've hidden a similar object somewhere out here, deep, and we need your dolphin to recover it."

"Is it dangerous?" Cory asked. "I need to know if it could hurt Kaj."

"It cannot." Landon said. He wasn't going to give Cory and Noah any more information than he needed to.

"Okay," Noah said. "We'll need to get it in the water, so Kaj can get a look at it."

Noah helped Landon hoist the minisub overboard, where it hung from chains off the bottom of the boat about a foot underwater. Cory attached a small device to Kaj's dorsal fin, an underwater camera with a short-range transmitter, so they could see what Kaj saw as he swam.

Once they flipped on their rugged laptop computer, they got a fin's-eye view of themselves. Cory raised his arm and Kaj slid himself right off his pad into the ocean. He circled the boat and checked out the strange new object hanging off its side. He bumped it with the hard bone in the tip of his snout, called the *rostrum*, which is like a dolphin's index finger. Kaj used it for touching, for pointing, and for playing.

On the screen, they saw the bottom of their own boat and the blue void beyond, dappled with sunlight that bent and danced through the water.

At Cory's whistle, Kaj came back to the surface and stuck his head out of the water alongside the boat. Cory gave him a fish, and then got ready to blow the whistle again to tell Kaj to search. Landon stopped him.

"No whistles," he said. "We're going to need to do this silently."

Cory looked at Noah and raised his eyebrows. The whistle was an effective tool for dolphin training. They'd spent the past year developing a series of noises that Kaj could hear — and understand — over long distances. Being told not to use the whistle was like being told to speak without using the word *the*. It was possible, but it was much harder.

Cory made a gesture for Kaj, raised his arm up and lowered it, then swept it in a circle, which told the dolphin it was time to search.

Kaj flipped backward beneath the surface again, circled the mysterious object once more, and then dove. Cory, Noah, Landon, and the driver sat silently in their bobbing boat, waiting while the dolphin worked. The other boat floated about a hundred yards away, watching them.

"How long does it usually take?" Landon asked.

"That depends how close we are to the object, how deep it is, and how Kaj is feeling today," said Cory. "He's a living animal, with a mind of his own."

"But you're confident in his training?"

"Yes," Cory and Noah said at the same time. If there was one thing they knew, it was that Kaj was the best. If this thing could be found, Kaj could find it.

Dolphins could not only locate objects underwater, they could use their echolocation to almost *see through* objects. People still didn't fully understand how it worked, but the dolphin sent out its clicks and whistles underwater and the sound waves bounced off objects and returned to the dolphin. Somehow, the different speeds of sound waves returning told the dolphin not only what an object looked like, but how thick it was and, sometimes, what was inside it. In the wild, they used this ability to tell if a member of their pod was pregnant, or, when they were in a fight, they could see through their enemy's skin to where his vital organs were and then target their attacks to be as deadly as possible. Compared to looking at a creature's heart through its skin, finding a black submarine on the ocean floor would probably be easy.

But it was taking Kaj a long time.

On the monitor, they saw the distant shimmer of a school of fish, the outlines of rocks and coral on the seafloor, the quick movement of something Kaj startled as he swam past. Mostly, what they saw was darkness. The water and the depth were interfering with the broadcast, and the farther away Kaj swam, the more the signal cut in and out.

After an hour, they couldn't see anything on the monitor anymore. They opened another window on the screen, which showed a map of the area. There was a red dot moving through the ocean. The tracking device in the camera sent a blip that told them Kaj was now miles away, but how deep, they didn't know.

Cory wanted to whistle to bring his dolphin back, but whistling was forbidden and he had no other way to call to Kaj over long distances underwater. All he could do was wait.

Landon wasn't talkative. He was making notes in a little notebook he'd pulled from his pocket.

"He doesn't normally take this long," Cory said to fill the silence.

Landon nodded.

"Is that sub covered with something that makes it harder to find with sonar?"

Landon nodded.

That explained it. The sub was made of some kind of stealth material that couldn't be picked up on radar or sonar, so it could slip into enemy waters undetected. Whatever the material was, it was making it harder for Kaj to find, too.

Suddenly, the picture came back on their screen. Bright light, flashes of sun, and then sky. Kaj was at the surface and it looked like he was jumping and racing extremely fast. The image was blurred with his speed.

After more than an hour of waiting, Kaj was back at the boat in minutes, and he popped from the water and tapped the hanging baseball with his snout.

He'd found what they were looking for, and once Cory gave the signal, he'd lead them to it.

Cory smiled and praised him and tossed him fish. Kaj clicked contently and rolled in the water, while Landon and the driver heaved the sub they'd used as a model back on board. Kaj swam over to check out what they were doing. Once the sub was back on, Landon waved an arm signal to his guys in the other boat, and then he told Cory to get Kaj moving.

Cory pulled out a device that looked like a yellow plunger. It was a marker beacon that Kaj could stick on the object when he went back to it again. Cory fit the device snugly on the dolphin's snout, then made another wave of his arms and Kaj spun around, and dove again.

The driver gunned the engine to follow. Both boats zoomed across the sea, the dolphin leading them to their target.

Only fifteen minutes later, Kaj had dived out of view and then returned to the boat, without the beacon. He tapped the baseball again, and they all looked at the laptop screen, where a little green blip repeated over and over, several hundred feet below. Cory gave Kaj another chunk of fish and signaled him to jump aboard, where he could get some well-deserved tongue scratching.

Landon raised his arm and lowered it, and suddenly, two guys from the other boat, in full deep-water scuba gear, slipped over the side and vanished beneath the waves.

They were back in minutes, with flotation balloons attached to a black object just like the one Landon had shown Kaj.

Cory smiled as the SEALs secured the thing on board their boat. A job well done. They all sped back to the USS *Stokes*.

Landon looked grim on the way, though.

He came to the stern and sat across from Noah and Cory, looking at them over Kaj on his mat. Kaj's eyes watched the Navy SEAL commander carefully, and Landon seemed intrigued by the look he was getting.

"It's impressive," Landon said at last, shouting over the engine noise. "But when we go for real tomorrow, we need to be faster."

"Is that thing the same as what we're looking for on the mission?" Cory asked.

"Almost," said Landon. "Except we won't be the only ones after it. And if the wrong folks find it . . ." Landon trailed off. He reached out and touched Kaj's head. "Let's just say this fish of yours is our best chance of preventing World War Three."

Cory caught his breath.

He didn't even think about telling Landon that Kaj was not a fish. He just looked at Kaj's gentle little eyes, and wondered how a dolphin could possibly be expected to prevent a war.

04:
IN THE WATER

THEY came back up alongside the towering warship late in the day. No other ships were visible in any direction, just mild seas and puffy white clouds in the sky. The air smelled of diesel gas and salt water.

Cory noticed right away that the water beside the big ship's hull was churning. Fins and teeth flashed off the starboard side, and he tensed as they motored past. There were at least twenty sharks in the water, a school of them — what kind he couldn't tell — and they were in a feeding frenzy.

Noah laughed. "Looks like our food scraps are making us popular." The sharks had smelled the leftover food that sailors dumped in the water. A ship the size of the USS *Stokes* couldn't exactly haul all its garbage around for weeks or months at a time, so it dumped what it could overboard, the stuff that wouldn't do any harm — rotted vegetables, discarded apple cores, and leftover scraps of meat.

All that food drew fish to eat in the boat's wake, and all those fish drew sharks to eat *them*. Once a school of sharks got into a frenzy, it lured others to eat with the smell of blood in the water. There was plenty of food to go around; the sharks were wild with excitement. Finding a navy ship to feed off of made it their lucky day.

The commotion made Kaj click from his mat. He opened his mouth, not for a tongue scratch, but to snap it loudly shut again. He was out of the water, but he was still trying to scare the sharks away.

It had no effect.

Cory wanted to calm Kaj down, but his own heart was racing. He knew he was safe on the boat and in a few minutes they'd hook their RHIB to the monkey lines off the side of the ship and haul it out of the water. He and Kaj wouldn't be anywhere near the feeding frenzy.

But still, he'd broken out in a cold sweat. His fear wasn't something he could think away. It was like a living thing, rising up in him, taking over his mind. He couldn't control it. His breath was short. He was panicking.

Their boat bobbed up beside the ship, and a hook lowered down to them.

"Little help, sailor," Noah said as he began hooking Kaj's harness to the crane and prepping the dolphin to be hoisted on board.

Cory snapped to and helped get the dolphin ready. Noah waved the signal to lift the crane, and Kaj rose into the air. Cory watched him rise and rise, then looked back down to the feeding frenzy in the water, near the back of the ship.

"You should be there when Kaj gets on board," Noah said. "We'll take care of the boat." He pointed

Cory to the long ladder hanging down the side of the ship. "Get climbing."

Cory took a deep breath and grabbed the flimsy rope ladder. It jostled and twisted as he climbed, but he made his way up toward the weather deck one rung at a time. He could tell that Landon and the driver were watching him. The SEALs were trained to climb a rope off the side of a ship with ease, even in the dark, even under enemy fire.

On a perfectly calm afternoon, Cory struggled. His palms were sweating. About a third of the way up, he made the mistake of looking down. He could make out the bodies of the sharks beside the ship, thrashing and rolling over one another, turning the water red with the guts of fish.

"Get a move on, McNab!" Landon shouted up at him. He was startled to hear the SEAL shout his name, and the surprise made him slip. He grabbed at the next rung on the floppy ladder, but it was too late. He was already falling.

The air rushed by him as he toppled backward. He had the sense to push off against the hull of the ship so he didn't hit his head, and then he felt himself slam back-first into the ocean with a splash. The impact knocked the wind out of him and suddenly, he was underwater.

He heard the roar of engines in his ears, the furious splashing of his own arms, and he opened his eyes, seeing blurry through the chopping seas.

The shock of the fall quickly left him, and the new panic set in. He was in the water and all those sharks were in the water. Would they know he was there? Would they come for him? How long would it take for them to swim to where he'd fallen in?

He couldn't tell which way was up anymore. In his ears, he heard the screams of his little brother when the great white snatched him from the surfboard. He was there again, in his mind, all the panic in his body screaming out, even though he knew he was on the other side of the world. The sharks were coming for him. They wanted revenge. He'd stolen his brother from their jaws and now they were coming after him.

He clawed for the surface, trying to get out of their territory.

A shark brushed against him. He spun around, but he saw nothing. He felt another hit his side. But where?

He couldn't see it, but suddenly, his arms were pinned against his body. The shark had him! He was being dragged under!

He tried to free himself, tried to punch the shark loose, but he couldn't move his arms. He needed air, but the shark squeezed him and dragged him and he couldn't escape it and then . . . he was in the light.

He gasped for breath and he saw the inflatable boat just in front of him. High above he saw Kaj in his harness, still hanging at the end of the crane. Cory wanted to scream.

"Get it together, zookeeper!" a voice shouted in his ear. "I got you."

Landon.

The Navy SEAL had him in his grip.

It wasn't a shark.

It was Master Chief Landon Charles, who had jumped in to rescue Cory when he fell. He'd panicked and thought the Navy SEAL was a shark. He'd thought up was down and man was beast and he'd lost it. He couldn't believe he'd tried to punch Landon, who was trying to save him.

Landon had helped him out of the water and back onto the inflatable boat, before Cory realized that the Navy SEAL had insulted him.

Get it together, zookeeper.

The words echoed in his head as the ringing in his ears quieted.

"You okay?" Noah asked him.

Cory just nodded. He looked back and saw that the shark frenzy was far, far behind them. He'd never been in any danger from the sharks. It was his own imagination that had betrayed him.

Cory looked up at Kaj, high in the harness, now moving again, and he blushed. Even the dolphin had seen him panic.

"We'll get you to the corpsman when we're on board," Landon said, referring to the ship's medical personnel. "Just to make sure you didn't hurt yourself with that fall."

"Aye aye," Cory said quietly, and was sure he saw the boat driver smirk. Landon gave the driver a look that Cory saw as clear as day. Landon didn't smirk himself, but neither did he seem to disagree with his buddy.

Cory had learned to read unspoken communication from all his time working with Kaj, so he didn't need it said out loud to understand what the Navy SEALs thought of him.

To the real soldiers, Cory was nothing more than a zookeeper.

He was already failing, and the mission hadn't even started yet.

05:
THE MISSION

BY the time they got back on board, Dr. Morris and her veterinary team had already moved Kaj to the clinic for a checkup.

While his dolphin was with the doctor, Cory was sent to the ship's medic for his own checkup. He was still soaking wet and burning with shame, but he wasn't hurt and he was quickly dismissed back to his duties.

He had barely changed into a dry uniform, when an ensign came to tell him that he'd been called to the briefing room.

The XO, Lieutenant Brown, stood at the front of the room, beside a screen with a PowerPoint presentation projected onto it. The entire SEAL team was already in the room, seated on padded benches. Some officers and senior enlisted sailors that Cory didn't recognize stood around the edges of the room.

What Cory did immediately recognize was that he was the lowest ranking person in the briefing room and that Noah, his boss, was not there.

The officers looked at Cory doubtfully. Master Chief Landon Charles turned his head, and it was the first time Cory had seen him without his sunglasses. His steel-gray eyes gave Cory a look that could've frozen lava, then he turned away again.

Landon's words rang in Cory's ear: *Get it together, zookeeper.*

Was that how they all saw Cory, a zookeeper in a uniform? Did they not want him on their mission? Was this the moment he finally found out what the mission was?

"EOD McNab," the XO called out across the small room, using the abbreviation for Explosive Ordnance Disposal, which was technically Cory's specialty as a dolphin handler, even though he had never actually disposed of any actual explosive ordnance in his entire career with the navy. He just helped the dolphin find it so other guys could dispose of it.

"Yes, sir," Cory said.

"You get your clearance from the corpsman? Shipshape after that fall?" the XO asked. Cory knew he'd turned red again. Everyone in the room, no doubt, knew about his fall and the panic that followed. Everyone on board the ship probably knew about it.

"Yes, sir," said Cory. "Shipshape."

"Good," the XO said. "Take a seat, and we'll get started."

Cory found the only open seat, which apparently had been saved just for him, right up front next to Landon. He could feel the SEALs' eyes cutting into him as he moved to the front of the room and sat down. He felt Landon tense beside him and shift his weight away a tiny bit, but Cory didn't dare look over in his direction. He kept his eyes fixed firmly on the presentation, and did his best not to imagine everyone laughing at him behind his back.

It really was amazing how much his brief time aboard this warship made him think of grade school.

"The briefing you are about to receive is classified," the XO continued. "You do not discuss it with anyone you don't see in this room right now." Cory looked around. He felt like the XO was speaking just to him. Everyone else in the room knew it already. The XO changed the PowerPoint slide, which brought up a picture of a small submarine, much like the one they had just been training with. "This is the Submersible Intelligence Platform. We call it the *SIP*. It is a covert intelligence gathering submersible that operates in extreme underwater conditions without detection by hostile monitoring."

"A stealth sub," one of the Navy SEAL guys said.

"Roger that," said the XO. "It is also loaded with some of the most top secret artificial intelligence on earth. It is programmed to function without controller input, to gather information on its own and to evade capture."

"So it's like a thinking robot?" asked the same SEAL. "Like the Terminator?"

A ripple of laughter went through the room. Cory imagined a killer robot patrolling the ocean and did not feel like laughing.

"More like a really smart weather balloon," the XO said. "The SIP is not armed." Cory was relieved, as the XO continued. "But it is missing. SIP mission control has not had contact with their vehicle for three days. It was monitoring ship activity in North Korean waters, here." He changed the slide to a map of the coast of North Korea. A red circle appeared over a patch of ocean with some coordinate numbers next to it. Landon jotted notes in his little pad.

"It goes without saying that the North Koreans are less than friendly to us at this moment in time," the XO said. "If we are found to have launched a submarine into their waters, they would consider it an act of war. If they were to capture this submarine, they would have access to some extremely important military technology that we prefer they not know about."

The XO looked over the room, made sure his point was understood. Cory knew that North Korea was one of the most isolated countries on earth. He knew that it was an enemy of the United States and that they had been trying for years to build a nuclear weapon. He had not known that the United States was sending secret submarines into North Korean territory to spy on them, and he figured that was the whole point. No one was supposed to know.

"Your mission is to locate and retrieve or destroy the SIP. EOD McNab" — Cory sat up straighter — "and his dolphin will locate the SIP, with the SEAL team in support. Once located, the SEALs will determine if the vehicle can be recovered and, if not, obliterate it. You will then return to the *Stokes*, which will remain in neutral waters."

Landon shifted again in his seat. He raised his hand, and the XO acknowledged him. "Sir, can we discuss rules of engagement for this mission?"

The XO nodded and changed the slide to another map. "The North Korean military will be all over your area of operations. Evasion is the name of the game here. You are not to be detected, understood? We cannot send in support without provoking a much larger conflict, and the capture of American special operations forces at this time would be a massive problem for Washington, so —"

"So don't get caught," one of the other SEALs said.

The XO nodded.

"Sir," Landon spoke up again, "I have concerns about the dolphin team on a mission of this nature."

Cory clenched his jaw. He stared at the XO, fighting the urge to look at the Navy SEAL next to him, even though he was certain Landon was looking at him.

"What are your concerns, Master Chief?" the XO asked, crossing his arms and rocking back on his heels.

"Sir," Landon said, "I don't believe EOD McNab

has the training or the experience to accomplish the mission directives."

"Which is why you will be at his side to assist, Master Chief," the XO said with a touch of annoyance in his voice.

"Sir, my divers can conduct search and recovery without the aid of the Marine Mammal Program," Landon said. "Another robotic submersible could certainly scour the area where the SIP has gone missing. We brought two of them on board with us."

"You deploy with the dolphin team," the XO said firmly.

"Sir," Landon spoke again. "I have concerns about the operational capabilities of the dolphin team."

"Operational capabilities?"

"Yes, sir," Landon said. "After training this morning, I believe the dolphin team could become a serious risk to mission safety."

He had said "the dolphin team," but Cory knew what Landon really meant. He didn't think *Cory* was up to the job. He thought *Cory* was a serious risk to mission safety. He thought *Cory* was nothing more than a zookeeper.

The XO exhaled slowly, rubbed his head, and looked around the room before locking eyes with Landon again. "Let me assure you, sailor, that there is no diver nor any robot in the navy's arsenal that can search as quickly, as quietly, or as effectively as a well-trained dolphin. If the SIP is still active, it is programmed to avoid human or robotic detection. It is *not* programmed to avoid dolphins. If it is inactive, sitting on the bottom of the ocean somewhere, it will be invisible to anything other than a dolphin's unique bio-sonar. The dolphin is our best hope for recovery and your mission is to support the dolphin team's efforts, understood?"

The other SEALs shifted in their seats now, embarrassed for their chief, who had just taken a pretty harsh scolding in front of everyone.

"Yessir, understood," said Landon.

The next hour was spent going over plans and locations, showing specifications of the missing submarine, and reviewing backup plans.

"You deploy at sunset," the XO said, "so you can hit North Korean waters at nightfall. Will Mark Six be ready by then?"

Cory didn't answer. He wasn't really listening. He was thinking about deploying on a covert mission with a bunch of SEALs who hated him.

"McNab!" the XO shouted.

"Sir, yes, sir!" Cory snapped to attention.

"Good," the XO said. "I'll see you off at eighteen hundred hours." He looked around the room once more. "Let's get this right. We're not going to start a shooting war on my watch, understood?"

"Yes, sir!" the SEALs all answered in unison.

"Dismissed," said the XO, and the meeting broke up. Once they were in the hall, Landon cornered Cory and jabbed a finger into his shoulder, pressing him against the wall, his face an inch from Cory's face. His breath smelled like Starburst candy.

"You keep yourself together and do your job out there," Landon told him. "I can get you and your dolphin home, but if you freak out on me, if you endanger my guys or my mission, I will lose you in the ocean so fast, even your fish won't be able to find you."

Landon didn't wait for him to respond, just turned and walked away, leaving Cory sweating against a bulkhead in the belly of the warship.

"A dolphin's not a fish," he whispered, once he was sure no one was listening.

06:
GO FISH

THEY launched at dusk and sped for hours into the darkness. The orders were to maintain total radio silence, so the two inflatable boats did not communicate with their ship, and they could only communicate with each other by hand signals in the moonlight.

One boat held six members of SEAL Team Six, along with weapons and their diving and demolition equipment. The other boat held Cory and Kaj, Landon, and the driver. Cory was the only one without a weapon. Even Kaj had his teeth if they ran into trouble.

Landon would help Cory with Kaj and make sure they stayed safe, while the driver navigated them into hostile territory. The other SEAL boat stayed behind them about a hundred feet, looking out for any ships on the horizon so they could steer clear.

Cory used the hours of dark driving to show Landon where Kaj's supply of fish was, and his favorite toys, and how to keep Kaj calm by pouring cool water on him and scratching his tongue when he asked for it.

"You stick your hand in its mouth?" Landon asked.

"In *his* mouth," said Cory. "And yeah. He loves it. Also, it shows that I trust him not to bite my hand off."

"Trust." Landon repeated the word, looking at Cory intensely. Their eyes locked, and Cory's throat felt dry.

Cory wasn't sure what Landon was thinking. Did he not believe that dolphins could understand trust? Was he telling Cory he didn't trust the dolphin? Or that he didn't trust Cory?

"I better show you the signal for getting him back on board," said Cory, breaking Landon's stare. "In case I can't signal him . . . in case anything happens to me."

Landon nodded. He didn't try to offer Cory comforting words. Even over the whine of their engine, Cory could hear the thumping of his nervous heartbeat.

As Cory demonstrated the basic gesture, Kaj bent his tail up in the air, showing off his wide gray flukes, which each had three jagged white stripes. The stripes looked like lightning bolts. Kaj waggled the flukes a little and opened his mouth, which was his way of reminding Cory to give him a tongue scratching. Kaj clicked at him by gurgling air through his blowhole.

Cory scratched Kaj's tongue. Cory was, after all, a very well-trained human.

"How do you know what he wants?" Landon asked.

"I don't speak dolphin, but dolphins are excellent at speaking human," Cory explained. "Or, at least, excellent at making themselves understood by humans. I wish we were half as good at it as they are."

Landon snorted. He clearly wasn't the philosophical type. He was a warrior and didn't have time to consider the deeper points of communication between species. He was focused on the mission at hand.

Landon went to talk with the driver, going over maps and notes from the briefing, and Cory went back to rubbing Kaj and waiting for something to happen.

Suddenly, Landon waved his hands in the air to signal the other boat. Their engines quieted to a low buzz as they slowed.

"We're in North Korean waters," Landon whispered. "We know they have their own listening equipment on ships out here, so we have to keep our volume down."

Cory nodded.

"We're about an hour away from the last known location of the SIP," Landon said. "That's where we'll deploy your fish."

"He's not a fish," Cory dared to correct him. "Dolphins are mammals. They breathe air and give their babies milk, just like people."

Landon cocked his head at Cory, sizing him up. He looked like he was about to say something, when, suddenly, water spouted up just off the starboard side. Landon swung his gun around to firing position and pointed it at the water. He held his free hand up in the air to signal a hold.

The other boat swung wide and Cory saw all its SEALs raise their weapons.

"Dolphins," Cory whispered. "It's just dolphins."

A pod of wild dolphins, about twelve of them, had come to surface around the inflatable boat and were now investigating it. One of them popped its head out of the water, and Kaj opened his mouth and began to squirm on his pad. There was clicking and squeaking. Kaj let out a series of whistles as he squirmed.

"What's going on?" Landon demanded.

"Kaj is introducing himself," said Cory.

"He's what?"

"Dolphins have names," Cory told him. "A series of whistles that are unique to them. They call it out to one another to say who they are, and they repeat one another's whistles back."

"What is the other dolphin saying?" Landon asked. His weapon was still trained on the wild dolphin, the barrel aimed right at the big lump of skull between the dolphin's eyes.

"I don't know what it's saying," Cory replied. "I only know the sound of Kaj's name. Like I said, I don't speak dolphin."

"Are they a threat to your asset?" Landon said. Kaj was trying to twist around to face the other dolphin, but the mat was holding him in place.

"Kaj is not my *asset*," Cory said. "He's a member of this team and he's my partner."

"Are. They. A. Threat?" Landon repeated firmly, no patience in his voice.

Cory rubbed Kaj's head to calm him. "I don't think so."

"Could they be North Korean spies?" Landon asked, his finger on the trigger.

Cory was shocked by Landon's question. "The dolphins? Spies?"

The wild dolphin's grin looked to Cory just like the grin on the dolphin that had saved him from the great white shark.

"Could the North Koreans have their own dolphin program?" Landon's gun stayed steady even as the boat rocked in the water. The barrel was pointed right between the dolphin's eyes. "Could they have trained dolphins like Kaj? Tell me now: Are these enemy assets?"

"No!" Cory whisper-shouted. "They're just curious. Dolphins like to see what's going on in their ocean. That's all."

Landon looked from the wild dolphin up to Cory and then back down the barrel of his gun again. He lowered it and signaled the other boat to stand down.

One by one, the wild dolphins bumped the small inflatable boat with the end of their snouts and then, one by one, they swam past, diving down into the dark and vanishing as quickly as they'd appeared.

When they were gone, Kaj calmed down and so did Landon.

"So Kaj has a name in whistles?" Landon asked, like he didn't believe it.

Cory smirked and then whistled his best imitation of Kaj's name. Kaj perked up, lifted his tail in the air,

81

and flapped his flippers. He returned the whistle, and Cory gave him a fish.

"Did he give you a name?" Landon asked.

Cory hadn't thought of that. "I don't know," he said. "I just know what the navy taught him. He probably knows a lot more than that."

"You think he knows he's in the navy?"

Cory shrugged. "I think he knows he's not like those wild dolphins."

"So he's more like a person than a fish," Landon said.

"A mammal," Cory reminded Landon. "And dolphins have always been close to people. There are, like, stories of dolphins and humans going all the way back to the ancient Greeks. Humans saved from shipwrecks by dolphins. Dolphins saved from being stranded on beaches by humans." He didn't mention his own incident with the dolphins who had saved him and his brother, how he owed dolphins his life. How they were the reason he hadn't quit the navy. "There's an ancient bond between humans and dolphins," he said.

"A bond," Landon replied. He had a way of repeating words after Cory said them, like he was weighing them in his mind, deciding if he agreed with them. "You always know you wanted to work with Flipper?" he asked.

"No," Cory told him. "It wasn't my first choice."

He braced himself, preparing to answer the question he hoped Landon wouldn't ask. He didn't want to admit what his first choice had been, how he'd wanted so badly to be just like Landon and his men but couldn't hack it.

Landon didn't ask, though. He let the silence settle back over them until they reached the coordinates he'd jotted down on his pad.

"Okay, McNab," he said. "Time for you and your *mammal* to do what you do."

He helped Cory open up the folded pads where Kaj was resting. Cory made the signal and Kaj, happy to be freed, shifted himself and slid right off the back of the boat into the water. Cory tossed him a fish, which he ate in one gulp. Then Cory gave him the signal for search and recovery, and the dolphin vanished into the pitch-black waters.

"You ever worry he'll swim away?" Landon asked. "Like he'll see his buddies in the wild and just make a break for it?"

"The navy hasn't lost a dolphin yet," Cory said. But he had to wonder, why would Kaj stay? Did he even know that he wasn't free? Was that what the wild dolphin had been whistling to him, telling him the real secrets of the deep, of freedom? Telling him that the humans were using him for their wars?

The thought was crazy, but Cory couldn't shake the feeling that the dolphins of the wild knew something he never could.

There was no time for philosophy, though. It was time to work.

Cory opened the laptop and clicked on the program that linked to the camera on Kaj's dorsal fin. The screen was black. He pressed a button to switch to the night-vision setting and the sea came alive in ghostly green. He knew he wasn't seeing things the way Kaj saw them, but at least he was getting a sense of what Kaj could see.

A school of small silvery fish darted away as Kaj swam by. The rocky ocean floor loomed up from the dark, the dolphin racing along it. Kaj's speed was astonishing to behold, and even Landon watched in awe over Cory's shoulder.

Kaj turned suddenly, for no reason the humans on the surface could see, then turned again. He bolted up toward the surface for a breath, and in the distance, Cory and Landon saw the quick splash as the dolphin dove again.

After a few more minutes, Kaj was too far away to see when he surfaced, so they had only the screen to rely on as he turned and twisted in the depths. At one point, there was movement on the screen, something large, and Cory tensed as Kaj pursued the shape, but it turned out to be nothing more than a drifting swarm of jellyfish, clumped together. The dolphin raced through them and their bodies glowed with phosphorescence. Kaj had probably made a snack out of a few of them. Cory wondered if the stinging jellyfish hurt him at all, or if their sting was more like the fizz in a soda to the dolphin's taste buds.

Suddenly, Kaj twisted and dove toward a dark hole in the ocean floor. It seemed like he couldn't possibly fit inside, but with a burst of speed, he turned sideways and slid into a rocky cave, racing along its jagged curves.

"He's after something down there," Cory said aloud.

A deepwater eel vanished into a crack in the wall, and Cory saw some sort of crablike creature scurry under a rock. Kaj moved along the narrowing tunnel with ease, until he burst into an open cavern, where he emerged into an air pocket for a breath, dove back down another narrow passage, and bumped his snout right into a dark object wedged between two rocks.

The signal jostled and the image froze for a second. The feed got choppy.

"There's interference from all the rock," said Cory, which, of course, Landon had likely already figured out. Cory just felt like he had to say something to fill the silence as they bobbed in the ocean, Landon leaning over his shoulder, waiting.

"That looks like what we're after," said Landon, shaking his head. "I can't believe he found it down there."

"He's an amazing animal," Cory agreed. "Looks like the thing is stuck in that crack."

"If we can get our divers to it, we'll blow it up," said Landon.

"And if you can't?" Cory asked.

"Kaj ever planted a bomb before?" Landon asked.

Cory didn't answer. Kaj was trained for search and recovery, not for demolition. But of course the dolphin could plant a bomb. He could put anything they told him to down there in that cave, but it didn't seem right to turn an animal as intelligent as Kaj into a weapon.

On the screen, the images came in bursts — the air pocket, and then the cave again.

"He's on his way back to us," Cory announced. He unstrapped the signal beacon, so that Kaj would be able to go right back to the trapped submarine and mark its location. The feed got smooth again and they saw the mouth of the cave looming up on the screen as Kaj swam straight for it as fast as lightning.

"That looks too narrow," Landon said.

"Kaj knows what he's doing," said Cory "He can make it through. He can tell if —"

Suddenly, the image vanished. The screen went dark.

Cory hit a key. Nothing. He clicked some icons. The image was still dark. He switched to the tracking-device view.

Nothing. There was no signal.

"What happened?" Landon asked.

"I don't know," said Cory. He looked up over the ocean. Moonlight flickered across the light chop of the waves. They made a gentle lapping sound as they slapped against the boat's rubber hull. Otherwise, nothing.

Cory waited. Had there been a collapse in the cave? Was Kaj trapped somewhere out there, in the deep, unable to breathe, slowly suffocating because Cory and the United States Navy had sent him on a mission he couldn't possibly understand?

"He needs to breathe," Cory said aloud. A dolphin like Kaj can hold its breath for about seven to ten minutes. Maybe fifteen, at most. Cory held his own breath and watched the seconds tick by on his watch.

07:
NIGHT FISHING

THREE minutes turned to four, then to five. The minutes stretched out so they felt like hours.

Landon broke the silence. "I know you wanted to be a SEAL."

"What?" Cory said. "How —?"

"I also know you didn't finish training," Landon added. "I did my research on you before this deployment."

"I —" Cory didn't know what to say. He knew his face had turned red, and he was glad for the darkness so that Landon couldn't see it.

"You should know being a SEAL is not for everyone," Landon continued. "There's no shame in that. We all find ways to serve."

"Why are you telling me this?" Cory asked. "Why would you even bring that up?"

"Because," said Landon, "I don't want you doing anything on this mission to try to prove yourself to us. I've seen guys do dumb things thinking we'll be impressed, and it never ends well for them or for us. I want *you* to focus on *your* job. The one you have, not the one you wanted. Do your job well and you won't have anything to prove to anyone."

"I'm not trying to prove anything," Cory objected. He knew that wasn't true. He desperately wanted to prove himself to the SEALs.

"Good," said Landon.

"Yeah," said Cory, defiant. He stared at Landon, and Landon stared right back at him. Cory wasn't sure what it meant. Did Landon know he was lying? Were they about to fight?

"By the way," Landon said. "You never thanked me."

"For what?" Cory replied.

"You never thanked me for pulling you out of the water. When you fell in."

"Is that what this is about?" Cory couldn't believe it. "You're mad because I didn't thank you?"

"It's only polite," said Landon.

The driver chuckled quietly to himself but didn't look back at them. Cory wasn't sure if Landon was just messing with him or if he was really offended. Cory always thanked his dolphin. . . . Had he really not thought to thank the human who had rescued him?

"I'm . . ." Cory stumbled. "I'm sorry. Thank you. Thank you for pulling me out."

Landon smiled. "No need to thank me. Just doing my job."

The driver burst out laughing, but Cory still wasn't sure if Landon was kidding or not. It was like they were in on a joke that Cory couldn't understand. He wanted to say something else, something to break the tension, but all of a sudden, Kaj's dolphin grin popped up to the surface beside the boat and his snout tapped the baseball.

Cory let out a small cheer. The dolphin's timing was perfect, and even better, he'd done exactly like he'd been trained. Tapping the baseball was the signal he'd found something.

Cory bent down over the side of the boat and patted Kaj's head, then tossed the dolphin a fish. Cory made another hand motion, lifting it straight up and opening his palm.

Kaj vanished below the surface, then popped up at the back of the boat and jumped onto his pad on board. Cory knew Landon was watching him closely, and he felt a little better about himself. Landon was right. He needed to do *his* job. Maybe he wasn't a Navy SEAL, but he could command a six-hundred-pound dolphin without saying a word. That was nothing to be ashamed of.

He looked at the camera attached to Kaj's dorsal fin and saw that it had been smashed beyond repair. Otherwise, Kaj looked unhurt.

"He must have run into the cave wall with his fin," Cory said, undoing the strap and pulling off the broken device. He was glad to have something to talk about other than his personal failings at SEAL training.

"I guess we'll just have to trust Kaj to lead us on his own without a camera," Landon said.

"Trust," Cory repeated. It seemed that Kaj had proven himself to the Navy SEAL. Cory wondered if that trust extended to him, too. From the conversation they'd just had, he doubted it.

He gave Kaj another fish, then placed the beacon device on the end of Kaj's nose. The dolphin would be able to swim right back to the SIP and attach the beacon to it. The SEALs would follow the signal and Kaj's work would, hopefully, be done. They'd take care of the submarine and be on their way back to the USS *Stokes* long before the sun ever came up. Cory began to relax. Mission accomplished.

He signaled for Kaj to go and attach the beacon, and Kaj gleefully leapt from the boat, sliding into the sea again. Landon waved his arm to tell the other boat it was time to go. Cory brought up a new window on the laptop screen, and, following the new blinking dot, the drivers took off after Kaj as fast as they could go without making too much noise.

Kaj was much faster, and the distance between the dolphin and the boats chasing him grew every minute.

Cory wasn't worried. He took off the baseball and stowed the pole. He slipped the ball into the pocket of his vest. He felt it was like a lucky charm. A souvenir from his first top secret mission.

No matter the distance, Kaj would return to them wherever they were. The dolphin was very good at finding his boat. Humans may be clever on the surface, but underwater, dolphins were the true geniuses. And about seventy percent of the earth's surface was covered with water, so it actually made sense to think of dolphins as the smartest creatures on the planet. Humans were only masters of the parts on land, after all.

Cory was lost in these thoughts, so he didn't really notice their boat slowing until the engines stopped and they began to drift.

"Down!" Landon whispered, swinging his gun off his shoulder.

Cory glanced over and saw that the other SEAL boat had moved away from them and the SEALs on board had also gripped their weapons. In the distance up ahead he saw Kaj come to surface for a breath, and then dive again, speeding farther and farther away from them. He couldn't see what had alarmed the SEALs.

And then a large fishing boat loomed up from the darkness, racing ahead on an intercept course with Kaj.

Its lights burst on, a spotlight scouring the water and blinking lights on the roof of its cabin and running lights along the deck.

"How in the world did that fishing trawler sneak up on us?" Landon snapped at the driver.

"They were running dark and quiet," the driver whispered back.

"Why would a fishing boat run quiet?" Cory wondered aloud.

Landon didn't answer him. The boat's spotlight settled on the water, illuminating Kaj just as he came up to breathe again. Cory saw a harpoon mounted on the bow and a man standing at the harpoon, ready to fire.

"They're going to shoot Kaj!" Cory cried out. He didn't know if North Koreans hunted dolphins — he didn't know anything about North Koreans, really, but he knew that some countries hunted whales for meat and oil, and whales were related to dolphins. Maybe people ate dolphins, too? Maybe the fishermen planned to eat Kaj! "We have to stop them!"

"Shh!" Landon snapped. He'd raised his weapon to aim at the fishing boat.

"We can't . . ." Cory searched for the words. "We can't let that fishing boat kill Kaj."

Cory saw Landon switch his weapon's safety off. "That's no fishing boat," he said.

08:
SHIPS PASSING

CORY watched, frozen with fear, as the big North Korean trawler swung around and accelerated to intercept Kaj.

Landon pointed his free hand at the antenna poking from the roof of the boat's cabin. "You see that? That's an old Russian military radio array. Fishing boats don't have those."

"Why are they after Kaj if they're not a fishing boat?" Cory asked.

"Well," said Landon, "they're probably *also* a fishing boat. The North Korean military disguises some of their ships, using them as fishing boats until they need them to be military boats."

"So which is it being right now? Why is it chasing Kaj?" Cory kept his eyes fixed on the spotlight in the water.

The SEAL boats had started moving again, slowly, keeping their distance. The fishermen — or whoever they were — hadn't spotted them. They were too fixated on the dolphin.

"I don't know," said Landon.

"We can't let them shoot Kaj," Cory said.

"If we give away our position, it will compromise the mission," said Landon.

"If they shoot Kaj, there won't be a mission!" Cory objected. "He hasn't planted the beacon yet. We don't know where the lost sub is, just that it's out there."

Landon seemed to consider it.

"Please," Cory said. "He's my partner. He may not be human, but he's on our team."

Landon took a deep breath and lowered his head

onto the stock of his gun. He raised a hand to signal his men on the other boat. They made some gestures and accelerated, drew closer to the trawler. They slowed just out of the glow cast by its lights. It was such a loud boat that Cory figured its crew would never hear the little engines over their own giant diesel.

From where Cory was, he could see someone on the bridge of the trawler shout something and he saw the man on the harpoon gun shout back. Then the spotlight moved and stopped on Kaj as he popped up for another breath of air. He was going very fast now, and Cory wondered if the dolphin knew he was being chased.

He dove, and the spotlight seemed to lose him. They scanned the waves with the light, and men on deck pointed and shouted at one another. Cory felt a moment of relief that they'd lost his dolphin. The trawler slowed, and the two boats in pursuit slowed as well. Landon still had his weapon aimed at the harpooner.

Suddenly, a second spotlight flashed on, slicing across the waves and landing on the second SEAL boat, lighting it up, bright as day.

Cory gasped, seeing that the other SEAL boat was empty.

It looked like a loose raft adrift in the ocean.

"Where did they go?" Cory asked.

Landon's eyes moved briefly to the water and then up again. All six SEALs were hiding underwater beneath their boat. Cory was amazed at how quickly and silently they'd managed that. They really were the best of the best.

"*Nugu ibnikka*?" a voice crackled over a loudspeaker. "*Nugu ibnikka*?" it repeated.

Landon looked at the driver, who apparently understood Korean. "They're asking who's there," he said.

Below the surface, Cory could make out the dark shapes of the SEALs in scuba gear gliding like sharks, fanning out and swimming toward the trawler.

"Are they going to board?" Cory whispered.

"We can't have them radioing back what they've seen," Landon said.

"They haven't seen anything yet," Cory said.

He looked at the men on the boat. None of them looked too threatening. It was hard to make out detail, but they were dressed shabbily, all of them rather small and skinny. One of them, standing on the bridge, had an old-looking rifle, but that was the only weapon Cory could see, other than the harpoon gun.

He saw the SEALs in the water getting closer to the boat. The fishermen hadn't noticed them.

"Are . . . are they going to . . . kill them?" Cory whispered.

"If they transmit that they have found an empty raft back to their base, these waters will be crawling with North Korean navy ships," Landon said. "Our mission will be compromised."

"But what if —" Cory started, but at that moment, with a loud splash and a barrage of squeaking, Kaj leapt from the water onto his mat, the beacon still on his snout.

At the noise, the spotlight swung through the dark and landed on Cory, Kaj, Landon, and the driver.

"Umjigimyeon sonda!" the voice on the loudspeaker yelled.

Cory saw the man on the harpoon bring the tip around to aim right at their boat, as another man on deck pulled out an AK-47 assault rifle.

"No!" Cory yelled, but it was too late. The man on the harpoon fired. With a loud blast, the harpoon shot straight for Kaj, helpless on his mat.

Landon squeezed the trigger and the muzzle of his gun flashed, but Cory didn't see what, or who, the master chief hit. He had already thrown himself at his dolphin, shoving all six hundred pounds of Kaj as hard as he could. He and Kaj slid overboard together, just as the harpoon smashed through the center of Kaj's mat and punched a wide hole through their boat.

As Cory plunged into the ocean beside his dolphin, he heard the loud pop of rifle fire, met by the quiet hiss of the silenced machine guns fired by the SEALs. Then he was underneath it all, in the silent ocean. It went dark — someone had shot out the spotlight above — and Kaj vanished with a flick of his tail, either spooked and trying to escape or continuing his mission to place the beacon on its target. It didn't matter which at the moment. Cory was alone.

He kicked his way up to the surface.

When he popped up again, only seconds had passed since he went under, but the firefight was already over. The fishing trawler was speeding away at full throttle, and his own raft was about twenty feet from him, sinking slowly.

To his horror, he saw the driver slumped over the wheel, unmoving, and at first, he didn't see Landon at all. Then he swam right into the master chief of the SEAL team, floating on his back, his gun resting across his chest, and a cloud of blood spreading out from a gunshot wound in his leg.

"We have to stop that boat," Landon said, rolling his head toward Cory.

"You're bleeding," Cory told him.

"Doesn't matter," said Landon. "We took out the communications, but they'll head for shore. We have to —" He started to sink, spat out water, and Cory grabbed him, kept him afloat. "We have to stop them."

Cory held Landon against his own chest with one arm, treading water with his legs so they both stayed afloat. He used his free arm to find Landon's wound, just below the knee.

"We have to get you out of the water," Cory said. "Can you swim?"

Landon nodded. "With your help."

Cory held him and together they started to swim for the other rigid-hull inflatable boat, which was drifting lazily away from them.

"Hughes," Landon said. "We have to get Hughes."

"The driver?" Cory asked. He realized he'd never even known the man's name.

Landon nodded again. Cory glanced at their sinking boat and the slumped driver. Even if he was dead, the SEALs would never leave one of their own behind.

"I'll go back for him," Cory said. "But first we have to get you out of the water and stop your bleeding."

Landon was losing a lot of blood, and that blood was spreading with the ocean current. The empty boat was now only about fifteen yards away. Cory swam as fast as he could, but he knew he could never swim fast enough.

Somewhere in the depths, he was sure, hungry sharks had just caught the scent of blood in the water.

09:
AFTERMATH

WITH one arm wrapped around Landon, Cory used the other to claw forward through the waves, fighting an ocean current. He swam with all his might, glancing occasionally back as his own boat sank slowly and the lights of the fishing trawler grew farther and farther away.

When he reached the other RHIB at last, one of the SEALs was back on board. He pulled Landon up, then helped Cory from the water. There was one other SEAL, in full scuba gear, lying in the hull of the boat, his eyes open toward the night sky.

He was dead.

Cory had never seen a dead body before. He couldn't tear his eyes away.

Less than ten minutes had passed since the first shots had been fired.

"Alvarez, what happened?" Landon asked the surviving SEAL.

"They were better armed than it seemed," said Alvarez. "They had some kind of commando team on board that boat along with the fishermen. The moment our guys went up, they engaged. Jackson was the first over the rail, and he took three in the chest." Alvarez finally looked down at the guy. "I took one in the side before I could get up there. Not too bad though. The bullet went clean through me."

Alvarez raised his elbow to show where his wet suit was torn. He had already packed his bloody wound.

"The others?" Landon asked.

"I missed a lot of what happened after they tagged me, but I got it on camera," Alvarez said, pointing at a small digital camera mounted on the front of the boat. "The rest of the team made it on board the fishing trawler, but I don't know their status. It looked like they were overrun. Whether they're captured or KIA, there's only one way to find out."

KIA. That stood for "killed in action."

Cory had never imagined, as a dolphin handler, that he would hear those words.

"We have to get Hughes," Landon said. The injured SEAL nodded. He started the engine of their boat. Cory was relieved not to have to swim back through the dark water alone. He was the only one of them who wasn't wounded.

Well, he and Kaj, but Cory had no idea where his dolphin had gone.

When they reached the other boat, it was over half filled with water. Hughes was still slumped over the wheel, up to his thighs in ocean.

"Go get him, McNab," Landon ordered Cory.

Cory cast a quick glance at the water all around the damaged boat, wondering how long he had before it went down, and before the deepwater sharks swarmed in. . . .

He took a breath and jumped from their boat into the sinking one, landing with a splash. He grabbed Hughes off the wheel and tossed one of the man's arms around his shoulders, hoisting him into a fireman's carry.

Hughes was a beast of a man, at least 250 pounds, and Cory's knees buckled under the weight in the bobbing boat. He fell, and both of them crashed onto the deck, waist deep in the water.

"Come on, McNab, get it together!" Landon barked.

He sounded just like the drill sergeant at SEAL training, shouting at Cory, urging him on, yelling at him to keep going when he didn't think he had any strength left. He'd quit then. He couldn't quit now.

The boat was almost below the waterline. A few more seconds and it'd go down; they'd both be in the sea. Cory saw a fin in the water, dark gray, darker than Kaj's. Then he saw another. They circled the sinking boat.

The sharks had come.

With a groan and a shout, Cory got underneath Hughes and lifted him once more, all the man's weight across Cory's back. He took one unstable step forward. Then another. Two more and he was at the edge, able to roll the big man off and onto the second boat, then to dive on himself, as the other one sank beneath the waves. All Kaj's toys and fish and supplies went down with it.

Cory lay faceup, catching his breath right beside Jackson's body.

"Hughes is alive," Cory heard Landon say. "He's breathing, just unconscious." Landon patted Cory's shoulder. "Nice work, McNab."

Cory sat up as Alvarez got the engines going again and pointed the boat in the direction the trawler had gone. They took off in pursuit at full speed.

"Wait," Cory said. "You're both bleeding." He looked at Landon's wound. They'd tied a bandage just above the knee, a tight tourniquet to stop the blood loss. "You could lose that leg if we don't get you to a doctor," Cory said. "We can't go after the trawler."

"We have to," said Landon. "If they have our guys

and get them to the mainland as prisoners, it won't just be this mission that failed. We shot their guys. They shot ours. The North Koreans will consider this an act of war."

"But we need help," Cory said.

"We have to maintain radio silence," Landon told him. "And if we get help now, this whole situation escalates. We send our ships, they send theirs. We try to get our guys back from the mainland, that's an invasion. North Korea has the largest military on earth. If this gets out of control, it'll be a war like you can't even imagine. It's up to us to prevent that."

"But —" Cory began, although he didn't know what to say. He was just a dolphin handler.

"You wanted to be a SEAL?" Landon said. "Well, welcome to the team, Petty Officer McNab. You're the tip of the sword now, and we need you."

Cory was speechless.

"I saw what you did for Kaj back there," Landon said. "You threw yourself in front of that harpoon for him."

"I owe dolphins my life," Cory said. "After I —"
He hesitated. "After I dropped out of SEAL training, a dolphin saved me and my little brother from a shark attack. I owe them everything."

"Well, then you got *me* out of the water," Landon continued. "And you don't owe me a thing. You've got heroism in your blood, sailor. I just need you to do a little more today. We'll make a SEAL of you yet."

Cory looked off the bow of the boat, catching the saltwater spray on his face. He couldn't see much of anything up ahead but tiny whitecaps on the water and the occasional twinkle of a star peeking out from the cloudy sky.

He looked back at Landon. The Navy SEAL had a hopeful look on his face. He was no doubt in a lot of pain, and at least one member of his team was dead. In spite of that, he was still ready to serve his country, his fellow SEALs, and his mission. He really was the best of the best, and now, he needed Cory.

Cory realized that it didn't matter whether he thought he could do it or not. This wasn't about proving himself. This was about being more than himself, leaving his doubts and his fears behind and rising up to meet the challenge, no matter how impossible it seemed.

Cory nodded. Ready or not, he would do this.

They sped into the night looking for traces of the trawler's wake on the water. It had shut down its running lights, so they couldn't see it on the horizon. Their small boat was faster, and they could catch up to the trawler, if only they knew which direction it was headed. Cory feared they had already lost it, and with it, the captured SEALs.

He scanned the horizon, searching for any signs of it.

"How do we even find that ship?" he asked.

Landon shook his head slowly. He didn't know. Alvarez kept driving, because to stop seemed like admitting defeat. If they stopped, their guys were gone. If they stopped, they couldn't prevent a war.

That's when Cory saw a burst of air and water shoot up from the surface about a football field's length away from them. At first he thought it was Kaj, coming up for a breath, but then he saw another plume of air and another. Fins broke the surface, then gray tails. It was a pod of wild dolphins.

Cory pointed, told Alvarez to catch up with them. Landon looked at him like he was crazy, but he nodded and Alvarez drove them toward the pod of dolphins, who were clustered just below the surface, not moving much at all, swimming lazily along. Alvarez slowed the boat as they approached.

"What are they doing?" Landon asked.

"Dolphins sleep with half of their brain at a time, so they can keep swimming and breathing and looking out for predators," Cory explained. "They're never fully asleep."

"Sounds like Hell Week," Alvarez said. The memory stung Cory and he felt, for just a second, the reminder that he was not like Landon or Alvarez. He was not a Navy SEAL.

As they drifted in their small boat among the pod of half-sleeping dolphins, Cory thought of the old saying about how it's best to "let sleeping dogs lie."

He wondered if the same was true with dolphins.

"What are we doing here?" Landon asked.

"If we're going to find that trawler, we're going to need Kaj's help," said Cory.

"We don't know where he is," said Landon.

"That's true," Cory said. "But we know his name. We'll just have to wake these guys up and ask them to make a call for us."

Landon nodded. He understood.

Everything depended on Cory's whistling.

10:
WILD DOLPHINS

THE boat drifted among the pod of wild dolphins. Their dark gray backs glistened beneath the surface. Some sank low while others rose up to blast air from their blowholes and take a fresh breath. Then they sank down again, making room on the surface for others, taking turns, clicking and whistling at one another. There were at least a hundred dolphins all around the little boat, a large pod, but not unheard of.

Cory suddenly grew nervous that he'd startle them and they'd go crazy, jumping and ramming the little rubber boat. A pod of dolphins this size could easily sink them. Dolphins had a reputation for being kind and friendly creatures, but they had a dark side, too. They were strong, they were fast, and they could be violent. There was a reason sharks were afraid of them. Dolphins had even been known to attack smaller dolphins just for fun, for practice at killing. Cory wondered if he was about to make a huge mistake waking them up and sending them after Kaj.

But he had no choice.

He leaned over the side of the boat and waited for a dolphin to rise up next to them for a breath. When it did, he patted it just in front of the blowhole, right where Kaj enjoyed being touched, and the dolphin woke. It twirled around in the water and shot its head up, looking Cory right in the eyes, clicking at him, sizing him up. The dolphin had a lot of scars and scratches across its head, far more wounds than a captive dolphin like Kaj would ever have. There was one deep scar that ran from its blowhole forward between its eyes and along the tip of its snout. It didn't look like another animal could have done that. Cory was sad to think that a human fisherman was probably responsible. The thought that any person could try to murder an animal as thoughtful as a dolphin made him shudder.

The dolphin with the scar poked itself higher out of the water, resting its large head on the edge of the boat and then opening its mouth wide to show all its glistening sharp teeth.

Cory recoiled away at first, then caught himself and looked at the dolphin again, clicking in its direction. Cory had the urge to toss the dolphin a fish as a reward, like he would've tossed to Kaj, but wild dolphins don't eat frozen fish like captive dolphins do. They're hunters. They use their teeth to kill what they catch.

And anyway, all Kaj's supplies had gone down with the other boat.

All Cory had to offer this dolphin was his trust.

He took a deep breath and stuck out his hand, shoving it right into the wild dolphin's mouth to scratch the dolphin's tongue.

"Hooyah," Alvaraez said. "McNab's crazy."

"Shh," Landon urged. "Let him work."

Cory smiled his appreciation at Landon and kept tickling the creature's tongue. Others had woken up now and come alongside the boat to investigate, sticking their heads up and eyeing the strange person in the boat with his hand in the mouth of their friend.

That was when the scar-faced dolphin shut his mouth around Cory's hand.

The dolphin's lips clamped on Cory's wrist, but it didn't snap down with its teeth. It just looked at Cory as if to say *your move.*

Landon jumped up on his one good leg, leaning heavily on Cory's shoulder, and pointed his gun at the dolphin. Alvarez nearly fell backward off the boat in surprise. Cory just stood there, unmoving, supporting Landon on one side, while on the other side he was gripped in the mouth of the giant wild dolphin hanging half out of the water.

"Stay calm," Cory warned Landon. "It's fine. He's just . . . testing me."

"Testing you?" Landon whispered, his anxious breath right beside Cory's ear.

"Testing me," Cory repeated and looked the dolphin in the eyes.

Cory had read about this behavior and been warned that some dolphins would do this. Their teeth are like little saw blades. If Cory were to yank his hand from the dolphin's mouth now, it would be shredded to bits. But as long as the dolphin didn't bite down, he'd be fine just waiting until the dolphin chose to let him go.

Or to drag him under.

Or to bite his hand off.

He kept looking at the dolphin. The others were watching, too. They swam around the small boat and glanced up at Cory as they looped around.

"Now it's your move," Cory said to the dolphin. He knew the dolphin wouldn't understand, but it felt awkward not to say anything. He waited.

And then the scar-faced dolphin opened its mouth and let go. Cory slowly withdrew his hand. Before the dolphin could splash back into the water and vanish into the pod again, Cory started to whistle.

His throat was dry, so it came out weird the first time, but it was enough to stop the dolphin from diving and get it to give him another look.

Cory whistled again, doing his best impression of the whistle Kaj used to identify himself. He repeated it. And after that he repeated it again.

Please understand, he thought. *You're the smartest creatures in the sea. Please understand what I need. Please . . .*

He whistled again and this time, the scar-faced dolphin whistled back, imitating it.

It sounded much more like Kaj when the dolphin did it.

Cory did it again and then the dolphin did it again. Soon, others had joined in the whistling, imitating the scar-faced dolphin who was imitating Cory who was imitating Kaj.

"I don't believe it," said Landon. "It's working!"

"I just hope Kaj gets it," said Cory.

"There are a hundred of 'em making that sound," said Alvarez. "Your dolphin would have to be deaf not to hear it."

"Or too far away," Landon suggested.

Cory shook his head. "Dolphins can hear over miles and miles of ocean. If he's out there, he'll hear it, but I don't know if he'll understand it. We never trained for this. Never even imagined anything like it."

"Can't train for everything," Landon said. "Sometimes you've just got to trust."

He patted Cory on the shoulder, and Cory knew that this time, that trust included him.

Suddenly, the dolphins stopped whistling. They blasted air from their blowholes and dove away, disappearing into the ocean as mysteriously as they'd first appeared.

"Uh . . ." Alvarez said. "What just happened?"

"I don't know," said Cory.

"Maybe they got spooked?" Landon suggested as Cory helped him back down again onto the deck.

Landon winced. Cory noticed how pale he looked. He'd lost a lot of blood. Landon was tough, even with a ruined leg, but if they didn't get him to the medics on board the USS *Stokes* soon, he was not going to survive.

"I don't know how long we can wait," Cory said. "You need to get to a —"

"What's that?" Alvarez called out, pointing over the starboard side of the boat.

Cory turned around and looked into the water where the SEAL was pointing. He saw dark shapes swimming up toward the surface. The scar-faced dolphin popped up out of the water again, and beside him, a smaller dolphin appeared, mouth open for a fish or a tongue scratching of his own.

"Kaj!" Cory cried out.

The scar-faced dolphin whistled once more, a different whistle, and Kaj returned it, a perfect imitation. Then the wild dolphin vanished into the sea, not even waiting for a thank-you or a good-bye from Cory. He guessed wild dolphins weren't so sentimental.

"I don't believe it," said Alvarez.

"Dolphins have memories as good as humans do," said Cory, smiling. He gave Kaj a tongue scratching and noticed that the plunger on his snout was gone. "I think Kaj remembered his mission. He placed the beacon."

Landon came over to look. "We'll get to that later," he said. "For now, you think Kaj will remember that fishing trawler?"

"I know he'll remember it," said Cory. "I don't know how we'll tell him to find it. There's only so much a hand gesture and a bunch of whistling can do. Like I said before, I don't speak dolphin."

"Dolphins follow sounds in the water though, right?" Landon asked.

"Yeah," said Cory.

"And they think of those sounds like names and locations?"

"Uh-huh," Cory said, not sure where Landon was going with this.

"Alvarez, we have playback on that thing?" He pointed to the camera at the front of the boat.

Alvarez nodded.

"If dolphins can find each other by sound, maybe they can find a boat by the way it sounds," Landon explained. "We recorded that trawler speeding off with that camera. Maybe we can play it back for Kaj. Just like giving a dog a scent to chase."

"We give him a sound!" Cory smiled, impressed. "You know, Master Chief, you aren't bad at this at all. We'll make a dolphin handler of you yet."

Landon laughed. "And stick my hand in a set of those jaws?" He shook his head. "I don't have the guts for it."

Cory laughed, too. Alvarez had unhooked the camera from the front of the boat and was wiring it into the radio for an improvised sound playback. Cory was amazed. Was there anything the SEALs couldn't do?

Alvarez noticed Cory watching and shrugged. "I like to fix radios at home," he said.

When the wiring was done, Alvarez turned the volume low and they listened.

At first, there wasn't much to hear, then the sounds of boat engines. Then shouting. Cory heard his own voice call out "No!", the pop of gunfire. Grunts and groans. And then, the roar of the trawler's engines speeding away.

"That's it," said Alvarez.

"Okay," Cory said. "Turn the volume up and we'll put the speaker in the water to play it for Kaj."

They lowered the radio speaker into the ocean and Alvarez flipped the switch to play the engine noise again. Kaj, hearing the strange sound in the water, went over to bump the radio speaker with his nose. He knocked it a few times, swam around it, and then simply hovered in front of it, just off the side of the boat. Alvarez played it again two more times, and the dolphin seemed to listen.

Cory leaned over the side and slapped the surface so Kaj would come back. He touched the dolphin's nose gently, held up a finger, and then made the hand gesture for searching.

Kaj hesitated.

"What's he doing?" Landon asked, the SEAL sounding truly anxious for the first time.

"He's thinking," Cory said. "This is totally new to him."

Cory stared at Kaj, and Kaj stared back. Their eyes locked on each other. Cory knew he saw something behind those eyes of Kaj's, an intelligence that was more than a set of instincts and trained responses. Kaj was a living being who could make his own decisions for his own reasons. Kaj worked with the navy and got his food from the navy and lived on the navy's boats and in its tanks and sea cages, but Kaj did not *belong* to the navy.

This animal was free.

"Please," Cory said aloud, knowing full well the dolphin didn't speak English. "Please," he repeated. "We need you."

Kaj slipped slowly back down into the water and swam back over to the hanging radio speaker. He knocked it with his snout once more.

"Play it again," Cory said.

Alavarez played it and Kaj appeared to listen and, with one burst of air on the surface, he flicked his tail and raced off ahead.

"Go! Go! Go!" Cory hollered, louder than he probably should have for their covert mission. They were still in hostile territory after all. Alvarez gunned the engine and they sped off after the dolphin, who stayed near the surface so they could follow, leaping from the water, cutting the waves with the speed of a torpedo.

"Look at this." Landon chuckled to himself through pale lips, resting his head against the boat's transom. "Couple of injured SEALs chasing a giant fish."

"A dolphin is not a fish, it's a —" Cory started.

"I know," said Landon. "I just wanted to see if I still had your attention."

"You've got it," said Cory.

"Good." Landon cleared his throat. "Because you need to listen close. When we find this ship, you're gonna have to board it."

"Me?" said Cory. "But I'm not trained for that."

"Your dolphin wasn't trained for this, either." Landon pointed at Kaj leading them on through the night. "You saying you're gonna let your partner do all the hard work?"

Cory glanced again at Kaj, then back at the injured SEALs, the blood on the deck of the boat, the weapons scattered about. The dead body. Getting his dolphin to find the fishing trawler was one thing, but boarding it? Cory didn't think he was cut out for that.

"You scared?" Landon asked him.

"I . . . uh . . ." Cory balked. He took a deep breath. Then he nodded. "Yes, sir. I am scared."

"Good." Landon smiled. "Shows you're not crazy. Fear keeps you focused. Fear is the best friend you can have, as long as you don't let fear stop you from thinking and don't let it stop you from doing what needs to be done. Understood?"

"Understood," Cory told him. He understood very well, in fact.

The wounded Navy SEAL sounded just like Cory's little brother.

11:
DON'T GET CAPTURED

AS fast as the boat raced along at full speed, the dolphin was faster. Dolphins were built for speed. The navy's work with them began in the 1960s, when some clever researchers thought studying dolphins could improve the design of torpedoes. They wanted their weapons to move through the water as swiftly and silently as dolphins, but the navy researchers quickly discovered that dolphins could do so much more than swim fast. That was how the dolphin program began.

Cory wondered, if word got out that he had invaded North Korean waters with his dolphin, would that be the end of the dolphin program? Would that be the start of a war?

He couldn't focus on those worries. He had to focus on the mission ahead of him. He watched Kaj swim. When the dolphin leapt, his gray back shimmered in the moonlight, and when he cut back into the water, he slipped in without a splash.

It didn't take long to catch up with the fishing trawler. The boat loomed up at them from the darkness. Lucky for them it still had its engines running or Kaj wouldn't have been able to find it, but the boat wasn't at full speed anymore. In fact, it had slowed to a crawl, and for some reason, it was turning.

"They're changing course," said Alvarez. He slowed their own motor to keep the engine noise down and to keep their distance until they could make a plan. Cory noticed that Alvarez was driving with one hand. The other was clutching his side where they'd bandaged his gunshot wound. Blood had soaked through those bandages.

At least Alvarez was still on his feet. Landon didn't even look strong enough to lift his head off the deck. But as gravely wounded as he was, his eyes were still alert. He asked Cory to prop him up so he could get a better look at the trawler.

Kaj swam on, right up to the big fishing boat, and he circled it, jumping and slapping the water, like when he'd played his high-five game in the tank on the USS *Stokes*. He must have figured he'd won whatever game they were playing by finding the engine noise in the ocean that matched the engine noise on the recording. Once his victory lap was finished, he swam back to their little rubber boat and stuck his head out of the water, mouth open for a fish.

"Sorry, Kaj," Cory said to the dolphin. "Nothing to give you but a tongue scratching." He did that, but kept his eyes on the fishing trawler to make sure no one on board had watched the dolphin's return or seen their little boat approaching. "It looks like they haven't noticed us," he said. "I don't see anyone on deck at all, actually."

"Me neither," said Landon. He pulled out some night-vision goggles and glanced through them, then confirmed what they had suspected. "It's just the captain on the bridge, steering. I don't see anyone else."

"Maybe they're all belowdecks?" Cory suggested.

"It *would* take the whole crew to guard four of my guys," Landon said, thinking aloud. "But this just doesn't feel right. Why are they turning around?"

Alvarez checked his compass. "They're heading south," he said. "Away from North Korea."

"Something's up," Landon said. "We need to get eyes on board to find out what." He looked at Cory. "You're our eyes."

Cory swallowed hard.

"There is only the one guy on deck," said Landon. "You should be able to slip by him."

"And then what am I supposed to do? Hijack the boat?"

"Not a bad idea," said Alvarez.

Landon shook his head. "Find out where my guys are. If you're able, create a distraction for whoever is guarding them. That should be enough. They'll do the rest. If they have been captured, I'm sure they've already got an escape plan worked out. They just need an opportunity."

"Yeah," said Cory. "But what if *I* get captured?"

Landon pushed himself up, wincing. He raised his index finger in the air. "First priority," he said. "Don't get captured."

"But what if —?" Cory tried again.

"Plan for success here, McNab, not failure," Landon told him. "If you're captured, you need to get uncaptured."

"That's easier said than done," Cory countered.

"You got that right," Landon agreed. He unholstered a pistol strapped to his good leg, and held it out to Cory.

Cory took the weapon from him slowly, eyes fixed on the black barrel. It felt heavy in his hand. It was wet, but the grip wasn't slippery.

"You know how to shoot?" Landon asked.

"I hope I won't have to," said Cory.

"Switch off the safety, point at what you want to hit, and squeeze the trigger," said Landon. "Simple as that."

"Simple as that," Cory repeated, feeling the weight of the gun in his hand. He'd never shot at anything before, never even been hunting. Could he really shoot at a person, even if that person was shooting at him?

The gun was heavier than its weight.

"Relax," said Landon. "Odds are, you won't have to use it." Landon gave Cory the leg holster and as Cory strapped it on and slipped the gun securely into its place, double-checking that the safety was switched on, Landon looked at the fishing boat, which had finished its turn and started to accelerate.

"Let's talk through it. How are you going to get aboard?"

"I don't suppose you'll drop me off?" Cory suggested.

"We can't get that close," said Landon. "You're going to have to swim it."

Cory looked sadly at the dark water, imagining the nighttime hunters just below the surface. He sighed.

Kaj was still waiting by the side of the boat, mouth open, clicking happily. He hadn't yet figured out there were no more fish for him. At least, not on this little boat.

Cory looked back at the trawler and then smiled. He realized he could solve two problems at the same time.

"I think I can hitch a ride," he said, patting Kaj's head. "And get my partner here a well-earned snack."

Cory put one leg over the side of the boat, then then the other, dangling his feet next to his dolphin.

"Here we go," he said, and slipped into the ocean, grabbing on to Kaj by his dorsal fin. Kaj let him hold on, and Cory stretched himself out along the side of Kaj's body, hugging the dolphin. Alvarez played the engine noise underwater once more, and Kaj took off with a mighty sweep of his tail. In a splash of water, with a deep breath of air, they went under, and Cory held on as if his life depended on it.

12:
OCEAN COWBOYS

THE force of the water pushing against him as they raced along below the surface nearly pulled Cory off Kaj's back. He clung tightly, squeezing himself against the dolphin's smooth skin. He pressed his face against Kaj's fin, tucking his chin to keep his head from being snapped back by the speed. His chest was tightening, hungry for air. He tapped Kaj, and Cory felt them rise up, breaking through the surface. Cory inhaled deeply. Kaj blew out from his blowhole. They dove again.

In spite of his fear, the thrill of racing on the back of such a powerful animal was greater than anything Cory had ever felt while surfing. With the gun strapped to his leg, he felt like a cowboy of the ocean with Kaj as his trusty horse.

They broke the surface again just off the bow of the trawler. Cory gasped, and Kaj went right up to the hull and tapped it with his nose, just like he'd been trained to do when he found what he was after.

There was no time to hesitate. They were in front of the boat, but it was speeding up and Kaj was letting it pass so he could play in its wake. Cory had to get onto the metal ladder off the side as quickly as he could. He let go of his dolphin and kicked furiously to keep the pull of the boat from sucking him under. At the same time, he reached out and caught the ladder as it passed him. The force of grabbing it nearly ripped his arm out of its socket, but he held on and hauled himself up with all his strength. He looked back and saw Kaj leaping alongside the boat. The entire adventure was one big game for the dolphin, even though the consequences for Cory were life and death.

He scurried up the ladder, hand over hand, not looking down, but he stopped just below the railing at the deck. He peeked up and didn't see anyone around, so he took a deep breath and swung himself on board. As soon as his feet hit the deck, he crouched and pressed himself flat against the wall of the cabin. He slid along until he reached a low porthole window, and he peered below into the dim cabin.

He looked down on the Korean men standing around, clustered together in two groups. There were eight guys who had AK-47 machine guns and camouflage jackets. Standing apart, the rest of the men wore shorts and flip-flops, and he figured those were the guys actually tasked with fishing. The guys with the machine guns were the commandoes that Alvarez had mentioned. They were the ones who would be most dangerous.

On the floor in front of the crowd of commandoes, Cory saw the four Navy SEALs squatting with their hands behind their heads. One of them looked like he'd been punched a few times — he had a black eye and a bloody nose — but otherwise they all seemed to be okay. They'd been stripped of their weapons, and it looked like one of the commandoes was interrogating them. The SEALs kept their mouths shut and their eyes forward. They appeared to be ignoring the man who was talking to them, but Cory couldn't hear a thing, so he didn't know if the man was even speaking to them in English.

Cory knew he couldn't crouch on deck all night waiting. He had to do something to give the SEALs a chance to escape. He had to get the guys pointing guns at them to lower their weapons or to move away somehow, long enough for the SEALs to turn the tables on them and take control.

Cory needed to leave this window and find where the trawler kept the fish it caught. He hoped they actually did some fishing on the vessel, or else his plan wouldn't work at all.

He skulked along the edge of the cabin, heading toward the front of the boat. There were large crates on the deck and he kept close to them, glancing nervously up to the captain on the bridge, steering the boat forward in the dark. The trawler still had its running lights off, which made it easier for Cory to move around unseen.

He glanced over the ocean again and tried to see back to their small rubber boat, but it was too far off. Landon and Alvarez wouldn't come close until Cory signaled them by firing his gun into the air. In the meantime, they'd keep their distance and watch through the night-vision goggles. Even though they were far away, Cory felt safer knowing that Landon was watching him as he moved around. It was like having a guardian angel . . . with a silenced submachine gun.

Cory couldn't tell what was in any of the crates on deck by looking at them, but his sense of smell told him everything he needed to know. As quietly as he could, he pried the stinkiest crate open and saw it was filled with big, fat, silver fish, packed side by side with big chunks of ice and sawdust to keep the fish from spoiling before they got to port. He wondered again at the point of a boat like this. The soldiers on board searched the ocean for invaders while the fishermen caught as much mackerel as they could? Cory was glad the United States Navy didn't make him do double duty as a fisherman.

Then again, he was now doing double duty as a Special Forces soldier, when in reality, he was nothing more than a zookeeper in a sailor's uniform.

He smiled at the thought.

He felt like one tough zookeeper.

He grabbed two of the frozen fish and shuffled to the edge of the deck. He glanced up to the boat's cabin once more, hoping the engines were loud enough that the captain wouldn't hear what Cory did next.

He whistled for Kaj and held one of the fish out over the water. The trawler's deck was at least twenty feet above the surface, but Kaj came slicing up out of the water in a mighty leap, snatching the fish from Cory's hand and swallowing the entire thing whole before he'd even hit the water again.

The captain hadn't seen anything, so Cory gave Kaj the arm signal he'd first used when he brought Kaj aboard the USS *Stokes*: It was time to do some tricks.

This time, he wanted the captain to notice. He wanted everyone on the boat to notice.

Kaj would have to be impressive. Cory whistled loudly, then ducked down behind one of the crates. He saw the captain peer out from the wheelhouse, just as Kaj made his first showy leap. The captain watched in awed silence as Kaj jumped as high as Cory had ever seen him jump, high enough so his silhouette hung in a perfect arc against the night sky. Then Kaj did a midair roll, pointing his flippers up toward the clouds and slapping them together, like he was clapping. He rolled his way to the water again, hitting with a splash.

The captain of the boat called out something loud, and one of the fishermen popped up from the cabin below. Then another came up. And another.

Cory pressed himself as flat as he could against the crate and watched the bow of the boat, holding his breath. No one was on the harpoon gun, so, for the moment, Kaj was safe. As the fishermen came on deck, Cory didn't feel so safe himself. He peeked out from behind the crate. None of the commandoes had come up. Yet.

Kaj did not disappoint. He popped back up from the ocean and did three midair somersaults, then slid back underwater to pop up on the other side of the boat and do the same again.

The fishermen called out excitedly. They whistled, and more of the men came out from belowdecks to watch Kaj perform. One of the commandoes, gun in hand, stepped out to watch. Another followed him.

The dolphin swam a rapid loop around the boat, jumping every few feet and hitting the water with a slap of his tail so that there was a huge splash, which nearly reached the guys at the railing. They all laughed and pointed, gesturing and shouting to encourage Kaj to try to hit them with the water. It was impossible not to enjoy such a spectacular show.

Cory figured it was time for the grand finale.

As Kaj came around again and leapt just in front of where Cory was hiding, he tossed the second fish. Kaj caught it in midair and plunged back into the ocean.

The men on board had seen the fish fly out from between the crates, and they cried out in alarm, turning toward Cory's hiding place.

Cory unstrapped the gun from his leg holster and switched off the safety.

Just as the commandoes on deck were rushing over to see who had thrown that fish, Kaj performed his last big trick of the show. He shot up out of the water and leapt right over the entire boat from one side to the other. His body glistened in the air. His fins barely cleared the railing, but he made it, crossing over and splashing into the water on the other side. Then he dove, swam under the boat, and did it again.

One, two, three, four times he leapt over the trawler and all the men stared, dumbfounded, soldier and fisherman alike. Even the commandoes who'd stayed below to guard the SEALs pressed their faces to the port-holes to watch the spectacle.

That was their big mistake.

Just as Kaj completed one more leap over the boat, Cory fired his weapon into the night sky. All the men startled, ducking from the unexpected sound.

At the same instant, the SEALs in the cabin below used the distraction to pop to their feet, kick the legs out from under their captors, and seize their weapons.

There was a flurry of shouts and Cory heard a man yell loudly in English: "Drop your guns! Now!"

The fishermen on deck hadn't even been holding weapons, they'd been so mesmerized by Kaj's perfor-mance. They didn't understand English anyway, but they put their hands up and surrendered.

The two commandoes shouted at the fishermen, pointing their guns at their own shipmates. Cory couldn't understand the words, but it was clear from their tone that they did not want the fishermen to surrender. He sprang from his hiding place and pointed his gun at the commandoes.

"Drop your weapons!" he shouted. The fishermen looked from the commandoes to Cory and back to the commandoes again. One of the commandoes leveled his gun at Cory, and Cory saw the whites of his eyes. It was kill or be killed. Cory squeezed the trigger, but before he could squeeze enough to fire, the man's body jolted. His gun clattered to the deck and he fell on top of it, still. The other commando threw his weapon down and put his hands in the air.

Cory noticed a pool of red spreading from below the man who had fallen. He was confused for a moment. He hadn't fired, but the man was dead. Then he realized what had happened.

He looked off into the night, but still couldn't see the small boat floating out there. Landon, however, had been watching, and hadn't hesitated to shoot.

The SEALs pushed their new prisoners on deck to join the others. When they saw the body of one of the commandoes and Cory, holding a pistol, standing in front of a half dozen kneeling men with their hands in the air, the SEALs all glanced at one another in surprise.

"Stop the boat," one of them called up to the captain, but he kept driving. The SEAL fired the gun he'd taken from one of the soldiers, putting a single bullet through the glass of the bridge windows right next to the captain's head. The captain got the message and shut down the engines.

There were nine fishermen on board and seven surviving commandoes.

"We surrender," the captain called out in English, coming down the metal stairs with his own hands over his head. The commandoes looked at the captain the way Landon had looked at Cory when they first met — with utter disgust.

Cory couldn't believe it, but he had just boarded and seized a foreign country's ship with four Navy SEALs, a single pistol, and a six-hundred-pound dolphin doing tricks.

Thinking of Kaj reminded him to go back to the crate of fish, pull out another one, and toss it over the railing to his loyal partner.

Kaj ate it gleefully as he swam circles around the trawler.

Alvarez drove up in the small boat and Landon, still lying down in the hull, called out to identify himself. "SpongeBob One, this is SpongeBob Actual," he said.

"Roger that, SpongeBob Actual," replied one of the SEALs on the trawler. "The Pineapple is secure."

Cory couldn't help laughing. SEAL Team Six were the toughest guys in the world, but they'd picked their code names for the mission from the *SpongeBob SquarePants* cartoon.

"What's the status of Squidward?" Landon called out.

"He's shipshape," the SEAL answered, and Cory blushed, realizing they were talking about him. His code name was Squidward, the grouchy octopus on the cartoon. But then he had to smile because they'd thought to give him a code name at all. He felt, for the first time, like he belonged.

"How are you doing?" the SEAL on deck called down to Landon.

"Been better," Landon called up. Cory leaned over the side and looked down at Landon. Even in the dark, even at a distance, Cory could see that blood had completely soaked through the leg of Landon's wet suit. His skin was so pale he looked like a marble statue. If Landon didn't get help soon, there was no way he would survive.

They still hadn't completed their mission to destroy the trapped robotic submarine, and the sun had just started to turn the distant horizon pink. The dawn was coming. They needed to move quickly, but the captain of the fishing boat had other plans.

"We wish to defect to USA," the captain told the Navy SEALs. "You see? I turned the ship for south! See? See?"

"Defect?" the SEAL nearest him asked.

"They want us to take them back to America," another SEAL said.

"Like, uh . . ." The SEAL thought it over. "They *want* to be our prisoners?"

"We want freedom," the captain said. "In USA." One of the commandoes spat on the deck and muttered something to the captain. The captain shouted back at him. Then he looked back at the SEALs and smiled. "We are not like these men. We want freedom. Not to be enemies. Friends. We want to be friends."

"That is *so* not in our mission parameters," the SEAL said.

"We can't send them home," another SEAL replied. "They've seen us. They know we're American. Letting them leave isn't in our mission parameters, either."

"So what do we do?" They all looked down to Landon, their officer, for an answer.

Unfortunately, he had fallen unconscious and couldn't answer them at all.

13:
ONE OF US

"WE cannot go back," the captain of the North Korean boat told them. His English was accented, but clear. None of the other men seemed to speak English, and the captain did not translate what he was saying for them. The North Korean fishermen stood quietly and waited, hanging on the sounds of speech rather than its meaning. "We will help you," the captain said.

"Help us?" one of the SEALs scoffed. "You're the ones who shot us up to begin with!"

"Not us," the captain repeated, a plea in his voice. "Those men shot you!" He pointed to the commandoes, still kneeling under guard from three of the SEALs. "We will help you." He barked orders at the fishermen, who stood and started moving to the ropes off the side of the boat, and the SEALs had to shout at them to stop and to keep their hands up.

"Your man is hurt," the captain said. "Bring him on my ship."

The captain had a point there, although the SEALs didn't really need his permission. It was agreed that the fishermen would help hoist the rubber boat on board and that Landon could be looked after more comfortably belowdecks. Alvarez could get his wound stitched up, too. The SEALs had their own medical supplies, and now they had a good space in which to take care of one another.

Cory and three of the other SEALs were left to guard the commandoes, while the other tended to the wounded. Cory kept looking anxiously to the cabin door, worried about Landon.

"If we go back home now," the captain told him, "we will be punished for the damage to our ship.

Punished for failing to keep our prisoners. Punished for wanting to be free. Our families will be punished."

Cory knew that people in North Korea were sent to labor camps and prisons for all kinds of reasons — saying the wrong thing about the government, laughing at the wrong jokes, messing up on their job. He figured letting an entire team of Navy SEALs seize your fishing boat and escape would be considered a pretty big failure. These fishermen were in a lot of trouble if they went back to their country after such a defeat.

"Won't your families be punished anyway if you don't come back?" Cory asked.

The captain scratched his patchy whiskers, thinking.

"If we are lost at sea, it will be better," he said.

"Lost at sea?" Cory asked. "What do you mean?"

"If they think we have sunk, then our families will be safe and we . . ."

"You'll be free," said Cory.

He looked out at the ocean again. He didn't know where Kaj had gone, but he was sure the dolphin was nearby. He couldn't help thinking of Kaj when he thought of freedom. These men on the boat didn't live in a free country. They were kind of like captives themselves in North Korea, and even though it meant surrendering to their enemy, giving up everything they knew, they wanted to come to America — "to defect" was the phrase the captain had used. To find freedom. They would risk their lives to be free. Meanwhile, Kaj risked his life over and over again, and always came back to his masters. Did he even know he wasn't free? Did he even know that right now there was nothing to stop him from swimming away and joining the wild dolphins? He would never again have to do tricks for anyone but himself.

Cory knew Kaj wouldn't abandon him. And he couldn't set Kaj free, but he could help these men get freedom.

"All your men want this?" Cory asked.

"Yes," the captain said. "They are young men. No children. They want new lives in USA."

"And them?" He pointed at the commandoes.

One of the commandoes said something, and the captain answered him.

"They will be celebrated as heroes lost at sea," the captain said. "Their families will be rewarded. They will cooperate."

"Wait a minute," Cory instructed him. He went to talk to the SEALs still on deck.

"I know what to do," he told them. "We can't send these guys back and we can't let them go."

"There's another option," one of the SEALs said gravely. He patted his gun. "No one would ever know." The other guys shook their heads. One looked down at his feet. "What other choice do we have?" the guy continued. "I don't like the idea either, but letting them go could start a war. A lot more people will die."

"Listen," Cory pleaded. "I know how we can complete our mission and help these guys defect to America without anybody else getting killed."

"Oh, you know how to do that, huh, zookeeper?" the SEAL scoffed.

"Can it!" a voice snapped at the SEAL. It was Landon, awake, being held up by an injured Alvarez so he could be out on deck. "McNab saved your butts and kept more of us from getting killed. Our mission is still a priority, and if he has an idea how to get it done without any more killing, I want to hear it."

The SEAL started to complain. "But Master Chief, he's —"

"He's one of us," said Landon. "Because I say so."

The SEAL nodded and turned back to Cory, expectant. Everyone was waiting for him. It was just like when he arrived on the base, all those sailors ready to do what he said. He hadn't asked to lead. He didn't even really want to lead, but leadership was what was needed, so he cleared his throat and laid out his plan. When he was finished there was silence.

"You think that'll work?" Landon asked.

"It will," said Cory.

"And Kaj can do it?"

"I don't think there is anything that dolphin can't do," said Cory.

"All right," Landon said. He looked toward the sunrise, which was just painting the horizon red. "Let's do McNab's plan and get ourselves back home double-time."

"Aye aye!" the SEALs said without any more hesitation. They had their orders.

They turned on the laptop from the surviving boat and brought up the program that would show where Kaj had planted the beacon on the missing submarine.

While the SEALs prepared, the North Korean captain explained the plan to his men in Korean. Cory watched the men go wide-eyed as they heard the idea, and they kept looking back at Cory and then at the ocean, as if Kaj were going to jump out again and eat them all. When the explanation was done, they all set to work, picking up crowbars and axes and ripping off big pieces of their ship.

Landon was set down to rest across the deck with his head propped up on a blanket. He watched the Koreans and the Americans at work together and shook his head in disbelief. Cory started cutting off chunks from the fish in the crates so he could share them with Kaj.

"Hey, Cory," Landon called out to him. His voice was weak. He could barely keep his eyes open.

"Yeah?" Cory came and knelt down beside him.

"This plan of yours is crazy," said Landon.

"I know," said Cory.

"Just so you know, for what's it worth, I'd have been glad to have you on my SEAL team." Landon squeezed his hand.

"I'm just doing my job," said Cory, smiling back at the wounded soldier. "Anyway, like you said, this plan of mine is crazy. And if it doesn't work . . ."

"It'll work," said Landon. "Like *you* said, that fish of yours can do anything."

"He's not a fish," Cory said with a smirk. "He's a mammal."

"No." Landon smiled widely. "That dolphin is a SEAL."

14:
DIVE-BOMBER

THEY lowered the small rubber boat back into the water. Alvarez was driving, even though he was injured, and a demolitions expert from the SEAL team came for support.

"Mike," he introduced himself, not offering a last name.

"Cory," Cory replied, shaking his hand.

"Uh, yeah," said Mike with a smile. "I know."

They had a cooler filled with fish, and they had the laptop so they could track the beacon that Kaj had placed. They also had a supply of C-4 explosive and detonators. Mike assured Cory that he was a qualified demolitions expert and could hook up the bomb without blowing them all to bits.

"Anyway, what are you worried about?" Mike asked him. "This plan was your idea."

Once they were free of the fishing trawler, Cory slapped the surface of the water, and Kaj's big shiny head popped up beside their small boat. There was no mat for him to jump onto, so he'd have to stay in the water. No chauffeur service for Kaj this time.

Cory tossed him another fish. He knew the veterinarian would be upset when they got back to the USS *Stokes*. This fish wasn't nearly as high quality as what the navy fed Kaj, but they had to make do. Kaj was working hard and needed to eat.

Cory's stomach rumbled. He realized he hadn't eaten since breakfast the day before. He comforted himself with the knowledge that if his plan worked, he'd be back on the ship by lunch. And if his plan didn't work, well, a rumbling stomach would be the least of his problems.

After Kaj swallowed the fish, Cory patted his head. He glanced at the screen, where a single dot blinked on the satellite image of the ocean. It was the beacon that Kaj had planted.

"How far are we?" he asked Alvarez.

"About forty minutes out," Alvarez answered. "Maybe less."

"We better move it, then," Cory said.

"Will your dolphin be able to keep up?"

"Oh, absolutely," Cory answered.

Alvarez shrugged and gunned the engine. They raced toward the signal, and Kaj jumped and swam in their wake. The fishing trawler followed, keeping up as well as it could, although it fell behind minute by minute. They'd have plenty of time to catch up while Cory and Kaj took care of the submarine. Cory didn't look back at them. He knew they wouldn't return to the USS *Stokes* without him and the others, even though it was getting more and more dangerous for Landon not to have real medical help. There was only so much that emergency field medicine could do.

When they reached the spot in the ocean just above the blinking signal, the trawler was a speck in the distance. It was making its way toward them, racing the sun, which now peeked just over the horizon. They were still in North Korean waters and they were losing the cover of night.

That was also part of Cory's plan. In order for the plan to work, an explosion had to be seen from far away. It had to be seen by the very enemy they had spent all night trying to avoid.

When they'd stopped the engines to drift in place, Kaj was there. The dolphin had to be exhausted, and there was still a lot left to do. Cory wondered: What would happen if he pushed Kaj too hard? Would the dolphin swim away? Would he work himself to death? Was it really right for Cory to put him through all this? Was it really fair?

Fair or not, it was what needed to happen.

Cory raised his arm and signaled Kaj to jump partway on board the boat. The dolphin leapt out of the water and perched on the gunwale on the edge with his flukes raised, like he was posing. The weight of the dolphin lifted the other end of the boat out of the water, and Cory feared they might flip. Kaj held still, though, and the boat steadied. The dolphin clicked happily where he perched, and Cory gave him another fish, then patted his side, rubbed his flippers, and did his best to help Kaj relax.

"Okay," he told Mike. "Kaj is ready."

Mike stepped up carefully next to Cory, trying to keep the boat steady. He held a harness of nylon webbing with a loop that could slip over Kaj's snout. A net hung below the loop and inside the net, they had wired a whole lot of C-4 explosive to a timer. They had to use a timer, because they didn't have a remote detonator that would work through the layers of rock and water between them and the submarine.

They used far more C-4 than was needed to blow up the damaged submarine, but obliterating the sub was no longer the whole point of the explosion. They also needed to create a big enough blast to draw the attention of the North Korean navy.

For the plan to work, Kaj had to plant the explosives. He also had to avoid blowing himself up in the process. The thought made Cory nervous. Kaj wasn't trained to carry bombs, after all. He was a search and recovery dolphin, not an armed weapon of war.

Cory continued to rub Kaj's side while the driver hooked up the explosives. Kaj watched Mike connecting wires and tying knots.

"It's okay, pal," Cory murmured. "You've just got one more job to do today. Then we'll get you home."

Home? Cory thought to himself. *Wasn't the ocean Kaj's home?*

Once the harness-bomb was attached, he and Mike stepped back.

Kaj's eyes met Cory's, and he wondered if the dolphin was afraid, too. It was so easy to look into those eyes and imagine the emotion behind them, but that's all it was: imagination.

Cory looked at Kaj but really only saw himself: his own worries, his own doubts, his own hopes. There was no way to know what Kaj really thought. He and

Kaj lived in different worlds. Kaj could never understand why Cory needed him to plant this bomb, just as Cory would never understand why Kaj did what he was asked to do. Humans had their reasons and dolphins had theirs.

For this dolphin, whatever his reasons, Cory was grateful.

He signaled to Kaj, and, with a jolt of his body, the dolphin threw himself back off the side of the boat and splashed into the water. All three men flinched as the front of the boat splashed down again, but everything was okay.

Kaj still had the harness on his snout. On the small screen, the beacon blinked, just below them. The trawler drew closer, only a few minutes away. Cory ran through the steps in his head.

He would signal Kaj.

Kaj would swim down to the submarine and plant the bomb.

Kaj would come back and they would all get on board the trawler and speed away.

The bomb would go off.

The North Korean navy would come to investigate, and they would find the pieces of their trawler that the fishermen had thrown overboard. They would think it was debris from the explosion, and the whole crew would be assumed dead in a terrible accident.

The fishermen and the Navy SEALs would go back to the USS *Stokes* to be debriefed, and Cory and Kaj would go home.

It was top secret, so there wouldn't be any medals, but if it worked, no one else would die. That would be reward enough for Cory.

He was about to signal Kaj to dive, when he stopped himself. He'd forgotten something. Something important.

He reached into the pocket of his vest and pulled out the ratty, wet baseball. Kaj's signal. Cory's lucky charm.

Cory grabbed a rifle from the deck of the boat and wrapped the barrel with waterproof tape, then hung the ball from the rifle barrel with another strand of tape.

"For Kaj," he said. "So he can tell us that the bomb is planted."

He held the rifle over the side so the baseball hung off over the water. Kaj noticed it and whistled.

"Time to play our last big game," Cory said.

He signaled Kaj to dive, and the dolphin twirled around, blasted a spout of air from his blowhole for a big breath, and dove, carrying the explosives with him.

15:
THE MOUNTAIN
BENEATH THE WAVES

CORY leaned on the edge of the boat, eyes on the dark water. The trawler approached, slowing its engines and drifting nearer. The fishermen and SEALs were all on deck, watching Cory watch the water.

Cory didn't see Landon, and his heart felt like a stone, sinking.

He held the rifle with the ball on the end out over the water and waited for Kaj to swim up and tap it. He watched the ocean just below the ball, as if he could tell by the rippling of the water when Kaj was close.

In truth, he could tell nothing. He just watched the water because he didn't know where else to look.

Every minute was the same length as every other minute, but expectation made time slow down. Cory thought he could count to himself to speed time up again. If he counted, he would know that a minute was really a minute, not an hour like it felt right now.

So he counted to himself while he waited for Kaj to come back. One minute, two minutes, three minutes.

Somewhere after ten minutes he lost count. Somewhere after the next ten he got worried.

Dolphins had excellent memories, as good as humans. Maybe better. Kaj was close to the beacon when he set off, and he had been there before. Kaj knew where he was going. He should have placed the explosives and been back by now.

Cory looked nervously at Mike, who looked nervously at his watch.

"It's been twenty-eight minutes," he said.

"And how long did we set the timer on the bomb for?" Cory asked.

"Forty-five minutes," said Mike. "So we'd have time to get to a safe distance."

"Do we still have time to get to a safe distance?"

Alvarez spoke: "Barely."

Cory thought of all the things that could have gone wrong: Kaj could have swum away. Kaj could have gotten lost, Kaj could have been attacked by a shark (although they didn't really attack dolphins; it was usually the other way around), Kaj could have gotten trapped.

Cory thought about the first time the dolphin went down to find the submarine. There had been an air pocket in the cave, so Kaj had probably taken more than one breath in the last twenty-eight minutes. But on his way out last time, he'd barely fit through the exit, bumping into the walls and breaking the camera. Maybe this time he'd gone a different way. Maybe the cave had shifted and rocks had come loose. Maybe Kaj hadn't fit this time.

Cory could sense it. Kaj was in trouble and needed help. He'd been there to help Cory. Cory had to be there to help him.

Even if it was extremely dangerous.

Even if he was afraid.

Kaj was his partner.

"I have to dive down there," Cory said. "I have to see if Kaj is okay."

Alvarez shook his head. "No way. Too dangerous. And you aren't a demolitions expert."

Cory ignored his objections. He propped up the rifle so that the ball hung over the water on its own, in case Kaj came back while Cory was gone. He started putting on the scuba gear from a small locker.

"I outrank you, Petty Officer McNab," Alvarez said. "I can order you not to go."

"Master Chief Landon Charles told you guys to follow my plan," said Cory. He tried to sound as serious and authoritative as he could. "This is part of my plan. Making sure my partner gets back safely."

"Are you even rated for deep diving?" Mike asked.

Cory was not rated for deep diving, but he'd made it through those first four weeks of the basic underwater demolition course. He had enough experience in scuba gear to go down and look for his dolphin. Kaj might be trapped, with enough explosives on him to blow up anyone within half a mile. It didn't seem like a deep-sea diver rating would matter much if things went wrong.

Cory put on the special diving vest, the tank on his back already. He held the breathing regulator in one hand and a mask in the other. He'd kicked his boots off and was looking around for fins to put on his feet. Mike shook his head, rolled his eyes, and started suiting up.

"You aren't going alone," he said.

"No," Cory told him. "I can't risk any more of your team. Kaj is my responsibility. No one else is going to endanger themselves."

"That's not how we work, Petty Officer McNab," Alvarez replied. "If you're a part of our team, then we are all responsible for one another."

Cory couldn't argue with that, and he decided it would be good to have another set of hands down there, especially another set of hands that had actually finished SEAL training. Mike was already suited up and ready to go.

Cory pulled the mask over his eyes, put the regulator in his mouth, and rolled backward off the boat with a splash.

The water was cold and dark, and it took Cory a moment to get oriented. The special tanks the SEALs used had rebreathers on them, so that the air he exhaled didn't escape as bubbles, which would rise to the surface, but instead was cycled back into the system itself and scrubbed clean. That way SEALs could stay invisible underwater for a very long time, and a special mixture of gases in the tank meant they could dive deeper than normal scuba divers.

In theory, Cory knew how to use all this stuff.

In reality, this was his first time trying the fancy equipment.

He had an underwater light attached to his wrist, and he flipped it on. Small fish scattered from the light. He pointed it down, and the beam diffused and vanished into the depths.

Mike was by his side in an instant, and together they swam down, clearing their ears from the pressure every thirty feet or so. The depth gauge on Cory's other wrist told him when they were at a hundred feet below the surface, then one-thirty. Then one-forty. One-fifty. And down and down.

As they swam deeper and deeper, Cory swept the light from left to right, looking for signs of rock or the cavern where Kaj could be trapped, but all he saw was dark blue and black in every direction. The water pressed in on him. He suddenly felt trapped, surrounded by open ocean. He had the panicked feeling of a person stuck in a tiny space with no room to move or breathe, no way to escape.

He saw dark shapes shifting at the edges of his vision, but when he turned to look he couldn't see anything there. He imagined deep-sea sharks, great whites racing in to snatch him from the black ocean and drag him away to a watery grave. He imagined Aaron again, all those months ago, blood on the waves as a shark tried to tear him apart.

In the hiss of his breathing he imagined the sharks

circling all around him now, hissing in shark voices: *revenge, revenge, revenge.*

He closed his eyes. Told himself to stay calm. Panic was the enemy here. Sharks were just a part of the natural world. They did not seek revenge. They did not think like humans thought. They could smell blood in the water, but not fear. Cory stayed afraid when he opened his eyes, but he did not let the fear make him lose control. There would be no more blood in the water today. Not his. Not Kaj's.

At two hundred feet below the surface, a shadowy giant loomed in front of them. Cory gasped through his breathing apparatus, thinking the shape was a huge whale or some unknown monster of the deep, but as they swam toward it, they saw it was a jagged mountain of rock, jutting from the ocean floor. A deep-water Mount Everest.

And as they drew closer to the mountain beneath the waves, Cory saw the sight he had dreaded seeing: Kaj, half sticking out of a collapsed cave entrance, both flippers pinned and the dolphin's head waving back and forth as he fought to free himself. The dolphin's mouth opened and shut with a loud snap. His little black eyes locked on Cory, and he stopped struggling. He whistled, and Cory recognized the sound. Underwater, the whistle was clear and mournful and sounded the way it was meant to sound. Kaj was greeting them with his own name in his own language. And it was beautiful.

I'm here, buddy, Cory thought, wishing he could whistle back something comforting. But this was Kaj's turf. Humans weren't meant to be down here at all, but they had sent Kaj and now they had to get him back.

Cory swam up to Kaj and rubbed his head to try to calm him. He could see where the rock dug into the dolphin's thick flesh, pinching him in place. In his struggling, it looked like Kaj had gotten himself wedged even tighter in the rock.

I'm so sorry, Cory thought. He knew *he* had done this. He knew he had caused Kaj to go into the cave.

He didn't know how long it had been since Kaj had taken a breath of air. Dolphins could go a long time without breathing, but eventually, they had to surface, or, just like a human, they would drown. This was already much longer than a dolphin could stand to hold its breath. Cory ran his hand over Kaj's head, felt the blowhole, and had an idea. When a diver underwater loses his tank, he can share the regulator with another diver, passing the breathing apparatus back and forth. When a human is drowning, like Cory almost drowned after the shark attack, another person can breathe into their mouth for them, forcing air into the lungs to keep them alive. As Cory had pointed out over and over again, a dolphin was a mammal, just like a person was, and there was no reason the same idea couldn't work.

He took the regulator out of his mouth, exhaling slowly to keep his lungs from collapsing under the pressure of the water, and he placed the mouthpiece over Kaj's blowhole. He pressed the button on the back, which purged the air from the hose at great speed and blasted a stream of air around the blowhole.

The dolphin squirmed and wriggled, and Cory felt a puff of air around the hand that held the regulator. Kaj had taken a breath. Cory took the regulator back, shoved it into his mouth, and inhaled. He had just bought them at least eight minutes before Kaj would need to breathe again.

Cory turned and waved for the other diver to come closer so they could try to figure out how to get Kaj free. Mike gestured at his face and then pointed to Kaj. Then he tapped his wristwatch.

Cory understood that the last part of the gesture with the watch meant they didn't have much time. The first part, however, was a mystery. The other diver repeated it, pointing at Kaj, and then Cory realized what he was saying.

Kaj did not have the explosives on his nose. He had done his job and planted them in the cave.

He had planted the explosives in the cave in which he was now stuck. If they didn't get him out fast, the explosion would blow them all to bits before Kaj even needed to take another breath. Drowning was the least of their worries now.

Cory looked at his own watch.

They only had six minutes left.

16:
A SCHOOL VISIT

CORY waved again for Mike to come closer. He floated beside Cory, studying the rocks that held Kaj in place. Kaj turned his head to look at the diver and let out a stream of clicks and whistles, which neither human could possibly understand.

Shhh, thought Cory. *Save your strength. Save your breath.*

Some mystic-type people thought that dolphins, with their giant brains, high intelligence, and mysterious language, were capable of reading minds. Cory wished that were true, because he had a lot he'd like to say to Kaj. He'd like to thank the dolphin for bringing him into the ocean again and for showing Cory what a smart and motivated soldier could do when he refused to give up, even when it was hard. Even when he was afraid. He also wanted to apologize to Kaj, for all the danger and all the trouble. He'd have asked Kaj if he really liked eating so much frozen fish.

But dolphins weren't psychic, Cory knew. They couldn't read minds. They were just creatures of the earth, with their own instincts and needs and thoughts. *This* creature in front of Cory, no matter what he could or couldn't do, no matter his special talents or high intelligence — this creature was Cory's friend. They didn't have to understand each other to love each other.

Cory decided that if Kaj was going to be blown to bits, Cory wouldn't let him die alone. Come what may, Cory would stay by Kaj's side.

Cory signaled for the other diver to get out of there, to swim away, but Mike just shook his head *no*. Together, they grabbed at bits of rock and started prying them loose. They moved as carefully as they could.

They didn't want to cause a further collapse, and they didn't want to cut or injure Kaj any worse than he was. Dr. Morris was already going to be pretty upset when she saw the state Kaj was in. *If* she saw the state Kaj was in.

They pried and jostled, pulling stones free with their bare hands. The deep ocean around them was cold as ice water, but Cory was sweating beneath his wet suit. Every few seconds, he checked his watch, rubbed Kaj's side to keep him as calm as possible, and tried to signal the other diver to swim away to a safe distance. Mike just kept working.

Cory pulled free one large, sharp stone that had pinned Kaj's back just in front of his dorsal fin. As the stone wiggled and slipped against his fingers, it dragged a deep line along Kaj's back. It had been stabbing into the dolphin, and as it came loose, Kaj unleashed a high-pitched whistle of pain. Then a stream of blood floated up from the wound the stone had made.

Almost done, Cory thought. *Just a few more.*

He checked his watch. They only had three and a half minutes before the bomb went off. Mike gave him a nervous look. He shook his head slightly, but this time it wasn't to say *I'm not leaving you*. It was to say *We won't make it*.

Cory doubled his effort. He pulled and pried faster and harder, with less care for injuring his own hands or Kaj's back. Another pained whistle. More blood in the water. Now Cory's hands were bleeding, too. And from the corner of his eye, Cory saw something swim past, investigating the scent. Then another something. He glanced over and shined his flashlight into the water.

This time, the movement was no illusion. His light caught the sleek body of a six-foot hammerhead shark gliding past. There was another right behind it, and another below and another above it. There was a whole school of hammerhead sharks, dozens of them, circling the undersea mountain peak. Kaj's blood rose from the cavern opening, mixing with the blood from Cory's hand, and in the glare of his flashlight beam, the blood rising from the mountain looked like a volcano erupting in slow motion. The sharks circled closer.

Cory stared one instant longer at their sleek bodies, their beady eyes, and powerful jaws. Then he looked at his watch again.

Two minutes, fifty-eight seconds left.

He ignored the school of sharks and the icy terror they sent up his spine as they drew closer and closer, and he focused all his energy on moving the next stone and the one after that, stone after stone, hoping he would move the one that would set Kaj free.

Suddenly, Cory felt something bump him from behind. Kaj opened his mouth and slammed it shut again, making a loud cracking noise, trying to scare the sharks away.

Cory didn't look behind him. He stayed focused on the dolphin. But he knew what was happening. Sharks use their bumps to test their prey, the way Cory's mother used to take a tiny sip of his soup when he was a little boy, to make sure it wasn't too hot.

Another shark came in and bumped him, knocking him into Kaj's side. The dolphin made another loud crack with the snap of his jaw as a hammerhead charged in. At the last moment, the shark turned away. Another came from the side, racing straight at Kaj. Cory put himself in front of his trapped dolphin, balled his hand into a fist, and slugged the shark in the nose as hard as he could.

The shark turned away. Cory checked his watch.

One minute, forty-nine seconds.

If the sharks didn't eat them, the bomb was going to blow them all to smithereens.

Three more hammerheads broke from their swirling circle and charged in, faster this time. Cory could see the rows of teeth in the vicious underbites as their mouths opened. They weren't afraid of Cory's fists anymore. Cory pressed his back against Kaj, blocking his partner with himself completely. He pulled another rock from its place without looking where he grabbed it from. He meant to hit the sharks with the jagged rock, but suddenly, with a high screaming whistle, Kaj broke free.

He burst out with a thrash of his entire body, spinning Cory around. A stream of blood traced Kaj's path in the water as the dolphin charged straight for the sharks. Kaj rammed one at full speed, smashing into its soft underbelly. Then he turned his body sharply and snapped his jaw onto the tail fin of another. The shark twisted and shook itself free, leaving a piece of itself in Kaj's mouth as it dashed madly down toward the dark. The shark Kaj had rammed began to drift sideways up toward the surface, lifeless. Kaj charged into the center of the school of sharks with a wild whistle.

The sharks turned on him, their school collapsing around the lone gray mammal. Over fifty hammerheads rushed forward to take on Kaj, who whistled and snapped his jaws, without scaring a single one off.

But frightening sharks had not been the purpose of Kaj's whistle.

Cory heard, over the roar of his own breathing, other dolphin whistles, loud and high, calling out in answer to Kaj.

And then from the dark behind the undersea mountain, a pod of dolphins a hundred strong charged, rising up to meet the sharks, and at the head of the pod, cutting the water with effortless strokes of its tail, the scar-faced dolphin slid straight through the beam of Cory's light. Wild dolphins to the rescue.

The sharks, panicked now, outnumbered and outmatched, scattered in every direction. The dolphins chased them off, and Cory looked to his watch again.

Thirty seconds.

The dolphins could swim away, but there wasn't enough time for Cory and Mike to make it to safety. Their eyes met, both of them acknowledging that grim truth at the same moment. They gave each other a respectful nod. They had made their choice, each willing to give his life for their mission and for Kaj, who was a member of their team. They regretted nothing.

Kaj swam back toward them, injured and surely running out of breath. He had to surface. He had to get away from the explosion.

No no no no no, Cory thought. He gave the hand signal for Kaj to swim away. Kaj didn't swim away. Cory motioned again. He wanted to scream: *Get away from here. Save yourself, you stupid, fearless fish!*

Cory laughed at himself, through tears in his mask.

Mammal, he thought. *You stupid, fearless mammal.*

My friend.

Go.

Instead, the scar-faced dolphin joined Kaj. A dozen others, too. They hovered in front of Cory and the diver, and for a moment there was nothing in the world but still and quiet. Mike and Cory looked at the dolphins, and the dolphins looked back at Mike and at Cory.

Cory and Mike had hardly spoken a word to each other on the surface. As they each looked at the dolphins in front of them, whose jaws were shaped into that mysterious smile, Cory wished he knew the other man better, although, perhaps, he thought, it wasn't so different from how he knew these dolphins. He didn't need to know them better. He already knew them at their best.

From inside the mountain below, came a rumbling. The water pressure changed around them and Cory closed his eyes.

The end had come.

The bomb went off.

17:
THE INDIFFERENT OCEAN

LANDON demanded to be carried on deck when he woke from sweating dreams to the sound of shouts.

Alvarez had returned to the fishing trawler.

Alone.

"It's not safe to move you, Master Chief," the SEALs told Landon, but he was determined and, now that he was conscious again, reminded them all that he was still in charge.

Two of the North Koreans carried him out on a canvas cot they used like a stretcher. They held him up so he could see. The sun had risen high and the other North Koreans were hard at work, throwing debris and pieces of their ship overboard. The sea churned beside the trawler, and among the debris, strangely, Landon saw the floating bodies of lifeless hammerhead sharks, one after the other.

"That'll puzzle the North Korean navy," Alvarez said. "But I gotta hand it to the dolphin handler . . . it's a pretty good plan. When the North Koreans arrive to investigate the explosion, they'll find all this wreckage and think the trawler had an accident. No one will come looking for these guys."

"And the unmanned sub?" Landon said.

"You should've seen the blast," said Alvarez. "From the surface you could see the flash of light, the rocks thrown out in all directions. Must've been over two hundred feet down and it was bright as lightning. No way there's anything left of that submarine."

"And . . . our guys?" Landon choked on the words.

Alvarez shook his head sadly.

Landon fought back tears. He had already lost one SEAL in the firefight. Now he'd lost another, as well as Petty Officer Cory McNab and his dolphin, Kaj. He had promised to get them home again, as long as they did their jobs.

They had done their jobs, but Landon had failed to get them home again.

Landon told himself that it had been a dangerous mission from the start. Those men knew the risks and they had died heroes. His guys understood when they became SEALs that danger was part of the job. Landon would recommend them for the highest military honors. He wondered if there was a way to have Cory honored as a SEAL posthumously.

Posthumously . . . meaning after death.

He sighed. It wouldn't be much comfort to his family, but it was the least Landon could do. Cory had mentioned his little brother. He hoped the kid could be proud of him.

"Motor up," he told Alvarez. "We have to get back to the *Stokes* before the North Koreans get here."

Alvarez bit his lip, nodded gravely. "Aye aye," he said.

Landon, dizzy and weary as he was, pushed himself high onto his elbows. He glanced briefly at the bloody mess where his leg had been tied off, and looked beyond at the merciless ocean. In time, nature would swallow all the evidence of the deeds they'd done here, and then what would be left?

The creatures of the sea were here long before mankind and our petty wars, he thought. *They will be here long after we're gone. What right do we have to bring our violence into their ocean, and to leave our dead behind?*

As the motors started and the boat began its turn south toward safer waters, he saw something in the middle distance, a churning, foaming patch of sea that he took at first to be a shark feeding frenzy in the aftermath of the explosion.

When something dies in the ocean, it becomes food for something else. In nature, death was a source of life. It wasn't kind, Landon knew, but it wasn't cruel, either. It was just . . . indifferent. But as they drew closer, he saw the slap of dark gray flukes in the foam and jets of air bursting against the pink morning sky.

It wasn't a feeding frenzy. It was a pod of wild dolphins.

"Belay that order!" Landon called. His voice cracked and hardly a sound came out. He repeated himself, forcing his voice from his lungs to shout as loud as he could over the accelerating diesel engines. "BELAY THAT ORDER! COME ABOUT!"

He pointed toward the pod. A dozen dolphins, two dozen, three dozen . . . all of them breaching and slapping at the water, churning the ocean so much it was visible from at least a mile away.

Landon remembered what Cory had told him: *I don't speak dolphin, but dolphins are excellent at speaking human. Or at least, making themselves understood by humans.*

"Binoculars!" Landon called out. One of the men brought him binoculars. He peered through them and got a closer look at the big pod of wild dolphins. They were leaping into the air and landing sideways with flips of their tails, making as big a splash as possible. They were blasting water high from their blowholes. And then he saw one of them, a still point in the center of the chaos, simply raising its flukes in the air, pointing its body up and down in the water.

With the binoculars still pressed to his eyes, Landon gasped. The dolphin with its tail up had three jagged white stripes on each fluke. The stripes looked like lightning bolts.

"Kaj!" Landon shouted.

He waved his arms for the captain to slow the trawler down as they approached the pod. When they drifted forward, Kaj flipped around, poking his head up, and stood high out of the water, clapping his flippers. Landon didn't know what the gesture meant, but when Kaj slid back down into the water, he saw what the dolphin was trying to show him.

Next to Kaj, clinging to one of the wild dolphins, there was a human figure in scuba gear and beside him, another floating faceup, being held on the surface by the gentle prodding of another dolphin at his side.

Landon didn't even need to shout the order. His men were already lowering the small boat to get their men out of the water.

As they were hauled on board, Alvarez was at their side in a flash. Mike was unconscious but breathing. Cory had his eyes open.

Landon's face broke into a smile when he heard Cory's hoarse voice speak out. "Mission accomplished, Master Chief."

Landon laughed. "Aye aye," he said, and ordered the trawler to head for the USS *Stokes* at full speed.

The entire pod of wild dolphins followed in their wake, jumping and playing in the waves the ship created. Only one dolphin stayed apart.

Kaj swam in front of the boat and led the way to safety.

EPILOGUE

DAWN patrol was still the best time of day to surf, and Cory sat astride his board as the waves rolled in.

Aaron was beside him on his own board as they watched the third surfer in their group rip a jagged cutback behind a wave, settling down on the smooth water again without falling. There wasn't even a hint of unsteadiness in his motion. The man lay down on his board and swam back toward Cory and Aaron.

"You guys gonna surf or just watch all day?" Landon asked when he reached them, catching his breath.

"Cory's afraid of embarrassing himself," Aaron joked. "You're twice the surfer he is with half the legs he has."

Cory balked at his brother's joke, but Landon broke out in a loud, sonorous guffaw, doubling over with laughter.

"I like your brother, McNab!" Landon said, patting his right thigh, just above the stump where it ended and the fiberglass prosthetic leg began.

It was true that Landon was a better surfer than Cory, even though he only had one leg. The other had been amputated by the ship's surgeon within an hour of arriving back on the USS *Stokes*. Landon had nearly died.

The rest of the SEAL team was in pretty rough shape. They took the body of the man called Jackson to the morgue. Alvarez and Hughes and Mike all had to go to the ship's infirmary, too. Cory was with them. He had to be monitored for head injuries and he needed stitches on his hand, but he was okay otherwise — thanks to the dolphins that had pulled him to safety.

The wild dolphins, led by Kaj, had not only saved Mike and Cory's lives, they'd probably saved the mission. The North Korean navy arrived at the scene of the explosion a short time later. If they had found the bodies of two American Special Forces operators, they could have accused the United States of launching an invasion. It still could have started a war.

Instead, the fishermen and the commandoes were presumed dead and would be relocated to America under new names; the USS *Stokes* could return to port; and the mission was deemed complete. The SEAL who'd died was given a medal in a top secret ceremony. Jackson was praised for his bravery and for his sacrifices, but the public would never know what had happened. For the men of SEAL Team Six, even their grief was deemed top secret.

At that same secret ceremony, Cory received a commendation for his role in the mission. He also received a new job. He would be the special operations liaison for the Marine Mammal Program. When the Navy SEALs needed a dolphin, he'd be the guy they spoke to.

As for Kaj, Dr. Morris got him in a mobile tank on board the USS *Stokes*, gave him vitamin supplements and a full medical exam and, other than some cuts and scrapes, determined that no serious damage had been done. The dolphin simply needed rest. He and Cory would be together in San Diego for an extended and relaxing vacation.

That was six months ago. They were back at work now, training every day. They spent the mornings playing and working on Kaj's search and recovery skills. Students from the local university took notes, while officers and other top navy brass stopped by to watch the exercises and ask Cory questions. The civilian advisor, Noah Hankins, was still technically Cory's boss, but after the top secret report of the mission came out, everyone in the know wanted to talk to Cory. The whole navy was excited about what dolphins could do for covert operations.

Cory wasn't sure if that was a good thing. He began to wonder if they should be using dolphins like that at all.

But it wasn't his place to decide. He did his job and cared for Kaj as best he could.

And on his days off, he got to hang out with his little brother and with Landon, who had left the navy and spent most of his days at the gym or the beach, recovering from his wounds and turning the loss of his leg into an opportunity to be stronger than he was before. In Cory's mind, that attitude was what made Landon a SEAL, even if he was retired from it for good.

"Why don't you show your bro a thing or two?" Landon suggested, and Aaron took off to catch another wave while Landon and Cory watched side by side. Cory looked over, seeing Landon's face silhouetted by the rising sun.

Just past Landon, Cory suddenly saw a fin slice the water.

A gray shape loomed beneath the waves and Cory found himself clenching his fists, but then it rose higher and he made out the form of a dolphin gliding beneath the surface, and then another and another. It was a small pod, come to play in the waves where the humans swam. Cory smiled to himself.

With his brother riding and his friend by his side and the wild dolphins below them in the waves, he knew he didn't have a thing on earth to fear.

AUTHOR'S NOTE

I should not surprise you that this story is a work of fiction. There is no such person as Cory McNab or Master Chief Landon Charles and, to my knowledge, no military dolphin named Kaj. If there were ever a top secret mission to find a top secret submarine in North Korean waters, I wouldn't know about it. I made all that up.

However, there really is a Navy Marine Mammal Program, based in San Diego. Until recently, the program was classified, but now we know that the navy works with bottlenose dolphins and California sea lions to guard ships in port, recover equipment from the seafloor, and detect undersea mines.

In fact, according to the navy's own statements, one rubber boat, one trained marine mammal, and two dolphin handlers can replace an entire navy vessel loaded with divers and doctors, expensive search equipment, and tons of fuel. The dolphins are given the same quality of care as dolphins in aquariums around the country.

In the story I've just told about Kaj, he was involved in very dangerous situations; however, in real life, the navy does everything it can to keep the dolphins safe from harm and out of combat roles. Sea mines, while dangerous for ships, are not designed to be set off by aquatic animals. The dolphins are trained to mark the explosives so that human specialists can disarm them. Dolphins have been deployed all over the world in this way, from areas currently in conflict in the Middle East to countries like Croatia, who have come out of their own wars and need to make their ports safe once more.

Dolphins are also used in the water the way guard dogs are used on land. A patrol boat with a dolphin can detect and intercept an attack from even the most well-trained swimmer. In fact, Navy SEAL trainees have been used to help the dolphins learn to catch illegal swimmers in the waters around naval bases, and even these elite soldiers are no match for the dolphins' echolocation.

In this story, I took the well-known skills and abilities of dolphins, as well as some of the cutting-edge research about dolphin memory and name recognition, and imagined its use in an adventure. The adventure itself was pure fantasy, and to my knowledge the navy would not deploy its mammals or its Marine Mammal Systems Operators in this way in real life. To make an exciting story, I took liberties with the dolphin program, with the navy, with North Korea, and with the Navy SEALs, but I took as few as possible with the dolphins themselves. They really are amazing creatures.

To learn more about the real Marine Mammal

Program, as well as the use and care of its dolphins and other sea mammals, you can visit the navy's Space and Naval Warfare Systems Command information page: http://www.public.navy.mil/spawar/Pacific/71500/Pages/default.aspx.

Or you can explore the recent inside look the navy gave to CNN, which includes videos of the dolphins at work: http://www.cnn.com/2011/US/07/31/marine.mammals.program/index.html.

PBS produced a brief timeline of the history of the navy dolphin program as well: http://www.pbs.org/wgbh/pages/frontline/shows/whales/etc/navycron.html.

To understand the history of human-dolphin relationships, the basic biology and training of dolphins, and the debate surrounding dolphins kept in captivity, I relied heavily on the book *The Dolphin in the Mirror* by Diana Reiss (Mariner Books), as well as *Dolphins in the Navy (America's Animal Soldiers)* by Meish Goldish (Bearport Publishing).

To learn more about the Navy SEALs, that elite fighting force, and get an inside look at how these brave men train, how they think, and how they operate around the globe, you could read *I Am a SEAL Team Six Warrior: Memoirs of an American Soldier* by Howard E. Wasdin and Stephen Templin (St. Martin's Griffin) or *Navy SEAL Dogs: My Tale of Training Canines for Combat* by Mike Ritland (St. Martin's Griffin).

Lastly, there is a lively debate about whether or not it is appropriate or moral to keep dolphins in captivity and to use them for military or even entertainment purposes. Dolphins are social creatures and need one another's company to survive. They communicate and remember and, from what we can tell, have rich and complex minds. We have learned a great deal from the dolphins we have studied in water parks, aquariums, and in the navy, but whether or not these programs should continue is a subject worthy of much more discussion, and there is no easy answer. The navy itself has decided to phase out the dolphin program beginning in 2017, both because of the expense of running such a complex program and because of the dangers to the marine mammals now that their service in the military is widely known. They will slowly replace some of the dolphins with mine-detecting robots, which are not yet as capable as dolphins but are far less complicated to care for. Even as the program is phased out, however, the dolphins will continue to provide protection to the navy fleet and the men and women who serve in port and at sea.

The dolphins currently in captivity cannot simply be released, as they would likely not survive in the wild. Provisions will have to be made for their retirement. Fortunately, the knowledge we have gained from marine mammals during their years of service has allowed humans to find new ways to protect dolphins in the wild. We have a long way to go toward responsible stewardship of our oceans and all the creatures in them, but I believe dolphins can be excellent partners in that effort, if they are treated with wisdom, generosity, and respect.

In that, I suppose, they are just like people.

■　■　■

Any and all errors in this book, whether they relate to the workings of the United States Navy, the training and care of dolphins, or the realities of SEAL Team Six, combat at sea, or relations with North Korea, are entirely my own. Everything I got right, I owe to the work of others.

This book would not have been possible without the help of retired Navy SEAL and journalist Kaj Larsen (yes, I named the dolphin after him), who offered basic facts when they were hard to come by, good-humored conjecture about my absurd plot, and generous encouragement, even when this endeavor seemed the height of silliness. Additional last-minute support came from the tireless Nicole Stokes. Her great-great-uncle Admiral Elmo Zumwalt already has a guided missile destroyer named for him, so I did what I could and gave her a warship in this book.

Allison Ginsburg, Manager of Marine Mammal Training at the National Aquarium in Baltimore helped probably more than she knows, and Dr. Jarrett Byrnes, of the University of Massachusetts Boston, marine biology professor extraordinaire, answered my questions when he could, and told more than I ever dreamed of knowing about the dark side of dolphins. I'm also grateful to my parents, who taught me to scuba dive, and especially to my mother, who spent many an hour with me at the aquarium teaching me to honor and love the ocean.

Thanks, too, to Nick Eliopulos, my friend and editor, who has worked unbelievably hard at a time when no one would have faulted him for coasting. And of course, I'm grateful to the rest of the Scholastic team, from Book Fairs and Book Clubs, to the rest of the editorial, marketing, art, and publicity teams, who work night and day to get the right book to the right kid at the right time. A special thanks is due to the copy editors and production team, especially Dan Letchworth and Emily Cullings, who have improved the quality of my work time and time again and who receive far too little glory for it.

I'm also grateful for all the men and women who serve this country in the United States Navy, for the work they do, the skill with which they do it, and the risks so many of them take about which we will never know. While many of their triumphs and their defeats remain top secret, my admiration need not. To all the sailors and SEALs out there, as well as the civilians who work with them, I say: Hooyah!

THE ACTION CONTINUES!

Meet Sly the Sea Lion in
Tides of War Book Two: Honor Bound!

01:
PARTNERS

THE intruder could come from any direction. He was in full scuba gear, deep below the rolling swells of the Pacific Ocean, and he had only one goal in mind: Don't get caught.

Felix stood in the small inflatable boat on the surface, scanning the ocean through binoculars. The day was bright and clear, with very little chop on the water, and good visibility in all directions. He glanced back at the *Prentiss*, the large US Navy Dock Landing Ship from which he'd been deployed . . . and from which he was being watched by senior officers visiting from all over the country.

Even though he didn't dare look back at them with his binoculars, he knew they were there, taking notes, discussing his performance, and preparing to report back on how he did and — more important — how his partner, Sly, did. It was really up to Sly to catch the intruder, after all. Sly was the one hunting in the dark ocean below.

Every few minutes, Felix looked down to the winch and the spool of cable by his feet. The cable unrolled steadily second by second, the towline stretching out into the blue abyss beneath the sun-dappled surface of the water.

"Come on, Sly, you can do it," Felix whispered to himself, willing his partner to succeed. He checked his watch.

Sly had been searching underwater for a while now. He'd popped his head up only once to take a breath, then disappeared again, and Felix had started to wonder what he was doing down there. Hunting for fish? Goofing off?

Having a sea lion for a partner wasn't the easiest thing in the world. Felix couldn't exactly explain to Sly that today's training exercise was especially important. That Special Forces operators and their commanders had come from as far away as Washington, DC, to watch. They were trying to decide the future of the navy's Marine Mammal Program. They were trying to decide what to do with sea lions like Sly and sea lion handlers like Felix.

Sly was an experienced search-and-recovery sea lion — one of only thirty-five sea lions in the Marine Mammal Program — but he was still an animal. Some days, Sly liked to let out his wild side, even when the boss was watching and even when the navy diver, who was pretending to be an underwater intruder, was doing his best not to let Sly catch him.

"You think he's taking so long because he knows your job is on the line?" Gutierrez asked. "Or does he just like the drama?"

Felix shrugged.

Gutierrez was the boat driver, a boatswain's mate, but he knew that it'd be easy for him to get a new assignment if they shut down the Marine Mammal

Program. They were in the navy. Everyone needed a boat driver.

As for Petty Officer Second Class Felix Pratt, he didn't know what he'd do outside the program. All his skills were related to training and taking care of Sly. If they shut down the sea lion teams, what need would there be for a Marine Mammal Systems Operator? Put another way, why would the navy need a guy who knew how to brush a sea lion's teeth?

Of course, Felix could do other things. He was a great swimmer. He'd competed on the US national swim team when he was in high school. He didn't make it to the Olympics, but he was faster than most guys he knew. Not as fast as a sea lion — they could swim up to twenty-five miles per hour — but still, for a person, Felix was like lightning. He'd been a lifeguard almost every summer since he was fifteen, so he knew CPR and first aid, and he was a certified scuba diver himself.

Surely, he thought, the navy would find a good job for someone like him if they closed the Marine Mammal Program. But he did wonder what would happen to

Sly. Would he be sent to a zoo or an aquarium? Released into the wild?

When a person imagined a seal in the circus balancing a ball on its nose, they were probably imagining a California sea lion just like Sly. If the military program was shut down, Felix feared Sly would be sold to a circus, although that wasn't really likely. But he couldn't be released into the wild, either.

Sly had lived his whole life in captivity with humans looking after all his needs. In their natural habitat, seals and sea lions like Sly fought one another for dominance in their groups, fought other groups for access to the best hunting territory, and did their best to keep from falling prey to the larger animals that hunted them, like killer whales and sharks. Felix couldn't imagine that kind of life for Sly. He was as much a navy sailor as he was a wild animal.

"Come on, pal," Felix whispered, checking his watch again. Navy sailors who can't do their jobs, don't keep those jobs for long. Even big, furry, fish-smelling sailors like Sly.

WHAT HAPPENS WHEN MAN'S BEST FRIEND GOES TO WAR?

IN AFGHANISTAN...

IN VIETNAM...

IN WORLD WAR II...

IN THE CIVIL WAR...